C000215999

Think Again!

MATT HAYDOCK

Grosvenor House
Publishing Limited

This book is published by
Grosvenor House Publishing Ltd
Link House
140 The Broadway, Tolworth, Surrey, KT6 7HT.
www.grosvenorhousepublishing.co.uk

A CIP record for this book
is available from the British Library

ISBN 978-1-80381-193-2
eBook ISBN 978-1-80381-280-9

To my grandchildren:

Ted, Layla, Abigail, Grace and Frederick.

Preface

Think Again! is the sequel to **A Work In Progress.** Although there is no need to have read that earlier work in order to enjoy reading this book.

Many of the characters mentioned in this novel also appeared in **A Work In Progress** and are wholly fictional. However, a few are genuine historical figures and much of what I have written about them is verifiably true. As for the bit that isn't? Well, who knows?

Acknowledgments

A number of friends made helpful comments after reading *A Work In Progress* and I kept them in mind during the creation of this sequel. I hope my friends will forgive me for not listing them all by name here. They know who they are. But there are two people I will mention. Firstly, my friend Graham, who gave me what is, I think, one of the best lines in the book. Secondly, my wife, Alex, who, with her encouraging and extremely insightful criticism, helped improve on the text. Alex also created the cover. Having said this, if the book still contains errors, or disappoints in any way, then that is definitely down to me.

THE PRESENT DAY

Day One - Monday

Tucked away just off the A22, fifteen miles south of London, is one of the country's most inappropriately named catering establishments. Furnished with nineteen sixties style formica-topped tables and bottom numbing steel tubular framed chairs, 'Lillian's Fine Dining' offers a menu that would make a dietician weep. The business is owned and run by the chain-smoking and redoubtable Lillian McLeash, known to her regulars as Fag Ash Lil, and her downtrodden husband, Charlie. Whilst Lillian remains very much in charge, Charlie, a wizened little man with very little to look forward to in life, goes about the job of serving customers and clearing tables, with the sad demeanour of a cruelly whipped dog.

Adding to the atmosphere is the constant loud din emanating from the radio, always tuned to BBC Radio 4, or as Lillian prefers to call it, The Home Service. There have been numerous appeals over the years for it to be re-tuned to one of the countless music playing stations, but all such entreaties have been rejected. Possessing an intense aversion to joy, Lillian has no desire to encourage finger drumming on tables, the tapping of feet or, even worse, the humming of a tune.

The establishment's clientele is very much a mixed bag. There are the regulars, mostly bikers, truckers and delivery van drivers. And there are the occasionals, people visiting for the first time, although there is a fairly high attrition rate amongst this group. Feeling they have been misled by the establishment's rather inappropriate name, many will quickly leave after taking just a brief glance at the menu. Some don't even hang around that long. A moment sampling the ambience of the place is enough to encourage their hasty retreat.

It was just coming up to seven in the morning and business was slow. The place would get busier later, but for the moment there were just a trio of regulars, and one occasional seated at a corner table well away from the others and looking rather out of place.

Lillian's Fine Dining is not the sort of eating establishment where one would normally expect to find the Commissioner of the Metropolitan Police Service, Sir Andrew Carpenter. He just happened to be driving passed and noticed it was open at a time when he was not only feeling hungry, but also in fairly urgent need of a comfort break. With few alternatives to choose between so early in the morning, he decided he had little option but to take the risk and give it a try.

Having just finished a greasy Full English, Sir Andrew was washing it down with a steaming mug of very dark tea and only half listening to the radio. When the seven o'clock news mentioned the name Gant, however, he gave it his full attention. It appeared that the BBC had a scoop, relaying a piece of news of which even Sir Andrew was unaware. Later that day, it was reported, the Department of Justice would formally announce that the trial of Sir Ted Gant would start in exactly one week's time.

The Commissioner was on his way back to London after a particularly enjoyable weekend's leave. Until that moment he had been in good spirits, but on hearing this unexpected news his mood suddenly changed. And, although not normally one for uttering profanities, under his breath he managed a whispered "Damn!"

A month had passed since the treachery of MI6 Deputy Director Sir Ted Gant had been revealed, thanks to the combined efforts of Sir Andrew and former army major turned priest, Chris Brazelle. It was a series of seemingly unrelated events that led to Gant's eventual exposure as a traitor. The process began when Brazelle paid an unscheduled visit to the Commissioner at New Scotland Yard. And it ended less than two weeks later, soon after Brazelle received a couple of unscheduled visits of his own. The first was from two armed men, falsely claiming to be Special Branch police officers, but they were very quickly disarmed and arrested. The second was from a far more dangerous individual, an international freelance assassin, known only as Orlando. He had arrived at Brazelle's cottage with just one purpose in mind, although, as it turned out, it was one he failed to achieve. Within just minutes of his arrival he was dead, blasted by a heavy bore shotgun at close range. And although the interior of Brazelle's cottage did not escape entirely unscathed, fortunately, he himself did.

Following Gant's arrest, both MI5 and MI6 were understandably keen to take part in his interrogation and the investigation that followed, but their requests for involvement were denied. Not knowing how deeply those intelligence services had been penetrated, Sir Andrew had managed to persuade the Prime Minister that the matter should remain exclusively under his control, at least for the time being.

Given the seriousness of the charges that Gant was facing, and the overwhelming mass of evidence pointing to his guilt, it was inevitable he would be remanded in custody whilst awaiting trial. Holding him in a prison, however, with the near certainty that his whereabouts would quickly become public knowledge, was considered far too risky. The international criminal organisation of which he had been a member had shown itself to be well informed, resourceful and ruthless. An attempt to free him was a credible possibility. Because of such concerns it was decided he should be kept hidden away in a safe-house until his trial began. An isolated farmhouse in Mid Wales was chosen personally by Commander Harris, Head of the Met's Witness Protection Unit, and its location was divulged to only a very small group of police officers. An even smaller group, reporting directly to Sir Andrew, was given responsibility for the prisoner's security and interrogation.

Gant was an arrogant and conceited man, but he was no fool. He knew he could not prevail in a court of law against the mountain of evidence assembled against him. He understood that his freedom could not come by way of some clever legal strategy created by a team of lawyers, however talented they might be. It could only come, he believed, through the illegal intervention of his former criminal associates. Confident they would not abandon him he waived his right to legal representation, refused to make a statement or answer any questions and waited for his liberators to arrive. Despite the best efforts of two of the Met's most experienced interrogators Gant had provided no information of value. Consequently, the investigation into identifying his former associates and their nefarious activities was not going well.

Convinced that Gant's resolve to stay silent would eventually fracture, Sir Andrew had hoped for more time for his interrogators to obtain some useful intelligence, but that had begun to look very unlikely. With the start date of his trial now set, Gant would soon have to be transferred to a prison, opportunities for his ongoing interrogation would then be far more limited and there would also be a big question mark over his security. His former associates had the advantage of anonymity, as well as a long reach that might well extend into any and all of HM prisons.

Barely an hour after leaving Lillian's Fine Dining, with the happy memories of his weekend's leave now pushed well to the back of his mind, Sir Andrew arrived in his office at New Scotland Yard. He was quickly joined by his PA, Mrs. Grace McAllister, who immediately asked if he had heard the news about Sir Ted Gant's impending trial.

"Yes I have. And it's not good," he told her, rather abruptly. "Postpone anything I have in the diary after two o'clock this afternoon and tell Chief Inspector Jenkins I want to see him straightaway."

Apart from Sir Andrew himself, Chief Inspector Ifor Jenkins was the only other police officer who had been involved in the Gant case from the very beginning. Equally well informed of the lack of progress in the ongoing investigation and already aware of the newly announced start date for Gant's trial, he entered Sir Andrew's office having correctly guessed why he'd been summoned. "I assume you're planning on paying a visit to the safe-house, Sir," he said.

"You've obviously heard the news. And your assumption is correct," Sir Andrew responded. "I'm going there this afternoon and I want you to come with me. Gant has been cut off from the outside world these last few weeks and won't have a clue as to what we might have discovered whilst he's been locked away. If we unexpectedly pay him a visit, looking rather pleased with ourselves, it just might unnerve him ever so slightly. Play it right, we might just get lucky and he'll let slip something of value. Quite frankly, anything at this stage, however minor, would be welcome. And it could be our last opportunity to get it. His arrogance and inflated ego are his major weaknesses, so they're the things to target. It's been quite a while since I played a bit of old fashioned copper's bluff, but I haven't lost my touch completely."

Sir Andrew was still wearing the civilian clothes he had arrived in, including, to Jenkins' great surprise, a brightly coloured tie.

"Do you intend travelling in what you're currently wearing, Sir?" Jenkins asked.

"Yes," replied the Commissioner, "although I'll certainly be changing the tie. I plan on being as inconspicuous as possible and I'd like you to do the same. And by the way Jenkins, have you still got that old banger of yours?"

Jenkins' feelings were hurt. "I'm not sure my five year old Volvo with only thirty thousand on the clock deserves to be called an old banger, Sir. But, yes, I still have it."

Sir Andrew smiled. "Good. We'll travel in that. And, if I remember correctly, it doesn't have a police radio fitted, does it?"

"No, Sir, it doesn't. Do you want me to requisition a portable unit?"

"Absolutely not," replied Sir Andrew. "And you can either travel without your mobile phone......" He paused for a moment and removed a small metal case from his desk drawer, ".....or you can put it in this Faraday pouch, along with mine. I want to eliminate any possibility that we can be tracked. Some people might call it overkill, but we still don't know exactly what we're up against. I'd rather be safe than sorry. And, incidentally, thank you for reading through that confidential report of mine. I had a chance to quickly thumb through it again myself over the weekend and noted the one or two comments you'd pencilled in. I doubt I'll ever need to resurrect it, but you never know. In the meantime I've lodged it somewhere safe."

Jenkins gave a nod of understanding. "Is there anything else, Sir?" he asked.

"Yes, just one more thing," the Commissioner replied. "Come armed."

As Jenkins opened the office door to leave, Mrs. McAllister entered carrying a number of envelopes and three small packages. "Happy Birthday, Sir Andrew," she said. "A number of cards have arrived for you. Seventeen so far, but I'm sure there will be more arriving later. And you've had three gifts: one from the Home Secretary; one from the London mayor; and one from me."

Sir Andrew thanked Mrs. McAllister and forced a faint smile. It was his birthday alright, but he was far from convinced it would be a happy one.

A few hours later, just as Sir Andrew and Jenkins were about to drive out of the underground car park at New Scotland Yard, Mrs. McAllister suddenly appeared. "I'm glad I caught you Commissioner," she said. "Another birthday gift has just arrived for you. It was delivered by special courier. The sender has obviously gone to some trouble to get it to you today, so I thought I ought to give it to you straightaway. It's gone through the usual checks, so it's perfectly safe to open." Mrs. McAllister handed a small parcel through the open car window and, as quickly as she had arrived, she was gone.

The package contained a rather expensive looking gold pen engraved with Sir Andrew's initials. He initially eyed it with a look of bewilderment, but, after reading the accompanying card, his face broke into a smile. Still smiling, he put the pen in his jacket pocket.

The safe-house and the conditions under which Gant was being held were far from commodious. Apart from thirty minutes each day during which time he was allowed outside to get some fresh air and exercise, and occasional trips to the bathroom, his universe consisted of just two upstairs rooms. There was a small bedroom, in which he spent his nights, and a slightly bigger room in which he spent his days, mostly undergoing interrogation. He was never left alone, except when he was asleep and even then he continued to be monitored via CCTV.

Throughout his time at the safe-house Gant had been without access to newspapers, radio, TV, phone, or a computer. And the windows of the two rooms in which he lived out his captivity were covered by steel shutters. To all intents and purposes he had been completely cut off from the outside world.

Even under the most generous interpretation of the law, the nature of Gant's incarceration was, to put it bluntly, at the very limit of what was legal. But, to put it equally bluntly, nobody appeared to care. Having waived his right to legal representation he had no lawyer to cry 'Habeas Corpus', his friends had all deserted him and members of his own family, even his wife, had chosen to adopt a low profile and gone to ground. Immediately following his arrest he had become persona non grata, a pariah and a complete outcast. Nobody wanted anything to do with him, except, perhaps, his former criminal associates. At least that's what he was hoping.

Just five police officers were based at the safe-house: Superintendent Michael Dorrian, the officer-in-charge and Gant's principal interrogator; Inspector Iolanthe Forbes,

Dorrian's deputy and fellow interrogator; and, a three man security team.

Sir Andrew and Jenkins were greeted by Dorrian and, after receiving a very quick briefing, went unannounced and unaccompanied into Gant's day room. The prisoner was seated at a table to which he was handcuffed, watched over by a single armed officer who Sir Andrew immediately dismissed, telling him to wait downstairs.

Gant was clearly surprised at the arrival of his two unexpected visitors. Whether or not he was in anyway unnerved by their sudden appearance, however, it was impossible to judge, as he made no comment of any kind and quickly adopted a look of bored disinterest.

Sir Andrew was the one to speak first. "We've come as bearers of good news, Ted. Well, good news from our point of view that is. Firstly, a date for the start of your trial has been set. It's next Monday. So it shouldn't be long now before you're officially told you're going to die in prison."

The Commissioner paused for a moment, waiting to see if there was any kind of reaction, but he wasn't too surprised when none came. Gant remained silent and simply maintained his look of utter disinterest.

The easy bit was now over. The Commissioner's next move would be far trickier. He was about to play a high stakes game of bluff. If he got lucky he might just provoke a reaction that would give him a snippet, perhaps a mere scrap, of information that could be helpful to his investigation. But the egotistical Gant had not become Deputy Director of MI6 through good fortune alone. An experienced, clever and calculating manipulator himself, he would not be easily duped into believing something that wasn't true.

As it turned out, Sir Andrew had barely got started before he was suddenly interrupted by the sound of shattering glass, immediately followed by a brief series of thuds and crashes, all coming from the room immediately below.

Six CCTV monitors stood together in the corner of the room where Gant was being held. Four were connected to cameras covering the area immediately outside and around the farmhouse, whilst the other two were connected to cameras positioned inside the building and focused on its front and back doors. Seeing nothing on any of the screens that might be considered unexpected or suspicious, Jenkins left the Commissioner alone with Gant and went to investigate. Downstairs in the hallway he was met by the three armed members of the safe-house's security team, all looking rather tense.

There were five doors leading off the hallway. One of the officers pointed his assault rifle at the only one that was closed and gave a nod in its direction. "The noise came from in there," he said. "It's used as an office by the Super and Inspector Forbes. I'm quite certain they're in there, but I got no response when I knocked."

Jenkins pulled his Glock semi-automatic pistol from its holster and began to gently push at the door. It didn't need to open very far before he could see the bodies of Dorrian and Forbes lying in front of the shattered window, each with a gaping wound in his skull. It was obvious both men were dead and, since it was equally clear that entering the room would not be a good idea, Jenkins reclosed the door.

On the face of it, the most obvious and urgent course of action would have been to call for immediate assistance, but this was much easier said than done. For reasons of security, none of the police officers had been allowed to have a personal phone at the farmhouse. There was a landline connected at the property, but it was quickly discovered that it had been cut, rendering the phone useless and removing any access to the internet. And the only police radio at the safe-house was in the same room as the bodies of the two dead police officers, in full view of the sniper. Even the mobile phones belonging to Sir Andrew and Jenkins were of no immediate use. They were still in the Faraday pouch and locked in Jenkins' car which was parked in front of the farmhouse, some forty yards away. Any attempt to get to it, with at least one sniper somewhere outside, would have been a near suicidal enterprise.

The members of the security team moved to take up different defensive positions inside the building, whilst Jenkins returned upstairs to quickly brief Sir Andrew on the situation.

Gant was clearly enjoying the police officers' obvious discomfort and for the first time chose to speak. "I have the solution to your problem, gentlemen. Whoever is out there has almost certainly come for me. But there is nothing personal in any of this. Just let me go and the danger to you all will immediately be removed."

"Your release will happen only over my dead body," Sir Andrew snapped back.

Gant curled his lip into an expression half smile, half sneer. "And no doubt that is what is being planned as we speak."

Sir Andrew remained with Gant whilst Jenkins returned downstairs and went into the kitchen at the rear of the building. As he opened the back door slightly his action was immediately met with a burst of automatic gunfire and he quickly slammed the door shut. His guess that the sniper at the front of the farmhouse was not acting alone was now confirmed to be correct. But just how many gunmen were there? And how long would it be before they made an attempt to enter the building?

As soon as those inside the farmhouse had realised they were under attack they had turned off the internal lights. Only the external security lighting had been left switched on, but when the electricity supply to the building was suddenly cut off, this too was extinguished.

The farm was not on the National Grid. Its electricity was supplied by a diesel generator sited in a small outbuilding at the side of the farmhouse, about thirty paces from the kitchen. If someone had just switched off the generator, then Jenkins knew exactly where they would have to be to do it. He carefully raised himself up to take a look out of the kitchen's side window. Although the combination of a dim twilight and a thin mist prevented him from getting a clear view of any potential target, he still managed to make out the vague silhouette of a figure exiting from the outbuilding. Taking aim he fired off several rounds from his Glock and the figure collapsed onto the ground.

Shooting at a target that was not clearly identified went against all of the firearms training that Jenkins had ever been given. But this was no training exercise. And he quickly put such thoughts out of his mind.

When there was no response to the shots he'd just fired, it gave Jenkins hope that the person he hit was the only gunman on that side of the building and a plan began to form in his mind. It was going to be risky, but, given the situation, he considered it to be his least-worst option.

The kitchen's side window was probably the smallest window in the farmhouse and Jenkins was a big man. But desperate situations call for desperate measures. Having forced himself through the undersized opening, he dropped to the ground outside. Although relieved to get out unscathed he didn't dwell for too long on thoughts of his good fortune, knowing it might run out at any moment, but moved quickly to where his victim had fallen. It turned out to be a tall, well-set male of about forty and although he was wearing several pieces of body armour, including a bullet-proof vest, none of this had saved him. Two of Jenkins's bullets had hit him in the head, whilst a third had struck and rendered useless a radio attached to his vest. The man was armed with a handgun, an assault rifle and a dagger, and it suddenly dawned on Jenkins that, apart from the dagger, every bit of his victim's kit, including the body armour and radio, was standard Met issue.

Despite concern that one or more of the dead man's accomplices might suddenly appear, Jenkins took a moment to search his victim's body. But he found nothing. There was no phone, no wallet, no identifying feature of any kind and he quickly moved to the next phase of his plan. In a wide arc, he circled round to the front of the building, intending to outflank the sniper who had killed Dorrian and Forbes.

Jenkins had been a police officer for long enough to have been involved in numerous events that had induced an adrenaline rush, although none as extreme as the one he was currently experiencing. And on more than one occasion, when an operation required him to carry a firearm, he had wondered how he might feel and behave if the need to use it ever arose. Tonight that need had arisen. For the first time in his life he had killed another human being and he was astonished at how unastonished he felt about it.

Now, yet again, and possibly not for the last time tonight, he found himself in a position where he felt it necessary to take another man's life. This time though, it would not happen through simply firing off a few rounds at some indistinct shadow in the mist. It would involve him making physical contact with his victim, before watching him die.

With a firm grip on the handle of the dagger he'd taken from his first victim, Jenkins silently crawled over the last few feet separating him from the killer of Dorrian and Forbes. Then, without a moment's hesitation, he pulled back the man's head and slit his throat. Some might say it was a cold blooded act, but Jenkins would almost certainly disagree.

Apart from the sniper rifle and the absence of a dagger, Jenkins discovered that his second victim was kitted out identically to his first. And a search of the man's body yielded nothing new.

Ever since Jenkins shot his first victim there had been only brief sporadic bursts of gunfire. As he completed his search of the sniper's body, however, automatic gunfire became almost continuous, with most of it appearing to come from inside the farmhouse. Although understandably concerned about the well-being of his fellow officers, Jenkins knew he must think and act strategically. For the moment that implied he should stay where he was and exploit his potential advantage. As far as any of the attackers knew, the only sniper in front of the building was one of their own, so they might not be too concerned at coming into his line of fire. And with the sniper rifle's military grade night-sight, the thin mist and fast failing light presented no great impediment to him fixing on any likely prey. He reckoned that even taking out just one of the remaining attackers would benefit the officers in the farmhouse, so he waited, hoping for a potential target to appear. As the seconds went by, the bursts of gunfire from within the farmhouse became less frequent, until they eventually stopped altogether.

Jenkins' impatience was growing, but he held his position for a short while longer and his restraint was eventually rewarded. From his current position he had a clear view into the room where the bodies of Dorrian and Forbes lay. He watched as the door from the hallway opened and two figures entered, both kitted out identically to his first two victims. They moved to stand in front of the shattered window and one of them waved in Jenkins' direction. Jenkins' response was to immediately take aim at the man's head and pull the trigger. The man fell, creating a moments confusion in the mind of his associate, lasting just long enough for Jenkins to take his second shot.

The sniper rifle had a very efficient silencer and Jenkins had shot through a window that was already shattered, so there was no sound of breaking glass. In fact the only noise that might have been heard inside the building would have been a pair of dull thuds as two bodies hit the floor in quick succession. Jenkins wondered if his luck was still holding. Perhaps there were only a very small number of attackers and the few who remained alive were out of earshot and unaware of what had just happened. He himself had now killed four of them. Just how many were left?

In the hope that his second victim was the only gunman positioned at the front of the farmhouse, Jenkins abandoned the sniper rifle and rushed forward towards the building, armed with his Glock and the assault rifle he had taken from his first victim. He intended that the shattered window through which he'd just fired would be his point of re-entry into the building, although he knew this might put him in double jeopardy. Not only would he be at risk from any remaining attackers, but he might also be in danger of being shot by one of his own men, assuming anyone was still left alive. As he hastily climbed in, he caught his hand on a piece of broken window glass creating a deep gash across his right palm. Blood quickly began to pour from the wound, but given his current situation he felt he had little option other than to ignore it and let it flow.

The door into the hallway was partially open. Looking out through the narrow gap that remained, Jenkins could just make out the lifeless bodies of the three police officers he had left behind with Sir Andrew. He gave out a sigh, but quickly returned to focus on his own situation as he became aware of moving shadows at the far end of the hallway, shadows that eventually transformed into human figures. Two more gunmen had exited from the kitchen and were moving slowly and silently in his direction.

Jenkins took a step back into the darkness and pointed his assault rifle at the small gap between the door and its frame. As the first of the two gunmen came into his line of fire he squeezed the trigger. His shooting was both accurate and deadly, but his target's automatic weapon had a hair trigger and a short burst of gunfire was returned. Reacting to a volley of several bullets striking his upper body, Jenkins stumbled backwards, lost his balance and fell, hitting his head, hard, on the wall behind. After this brief exchange the farmhouse fell into silence once more, until it was eventually ended by the creaking sound of a door slowly opening. The sixth gunman stepped over the body of his dead associate and looked into the room where five more bodies lay.

Alongside the corpses of Dorrian and Forbes, and Jenkins's third and fourth victims lay Jenkins himself, sprawled on the floor, a bloodied, lifeless mess. The left side of his face was covered in blood from a head wound caused by his collision with the wall; blood from the gash across his right palm and a bullet wound in his left arm was splattered over his body; and, there were several bullet holes in his sweater. Despite all of his injuries, however, Jenkins was in fact a lucky man. The gunman took him for dead just like all the other bodies lying around the room, turned on his heel and continued up the stairs to the room where Sir Andrew and his prisoner were holed-up.

The door to the room was shut and locked, obstructions easily overcome by a burst of automatic gunfire quickly followed by a vigorous back heel kick from a heavy boot. As the door flew open the gunman tossed a stun grenade into the room, before rushing in and instantly shooting a disorientated Sir Andrew in the head.

Gant was still handcuffed to a table at the far end of the room and the gunman waited in silence whilst he recovered from the effects of the stun grenade.

"I was wondering how much longer I would have to wait before you arrived," Gant eventually said. "But better late than never."

The gunman raised his pistol and pointed it directly at Gant's head. "Dink weer," was all he managed to say before a bullet from Jenkins's Glock smashed into the back of his skull and he fell to the floor. Dead.

For several seconds Jenkins stared in silence at Sir Andrew's lifeless body, before turning his attention to the corpse of his sixth victim. But it revealed nothing new. The gunman's kit, just like that of all the others, was identical to standard Met issue and there were no clues to his identity.

Jenkins left an inspection of his own injuries until last. After wrapping a cloth around each of his wounds, he pulled up his sweater to confirm that his bullet proof vest had saved his life. It had stopped four bullets, one of which had hit him dangerously close to his heart. Some bruising was inevitable, but thankfully nothing worse.

Ever since Jenkins entered the room, neither he nor Gant had spoken a word. Gant was the one who broke the silence. "That man was going to kill me," he said. No hint of smugness remained. It had been replaced by clear signs of shock and fear.

Jenkins pointed his Glock at Gant's head. "If you say one more word, just one more fucking word, I swear I'll put a bullet in your head myself. Because of you, six good men have died tonight. So keep your mouth shut."

Gant was left in no doubt that Jenkins was serious.

Despite not knowing whether or not any gunmen remained alive, Jenkins felt he had little choice but to take one more risk. In several mercifully uneventful stages he made his way to his car, bundled his still handcuffed prisoner into the boot and, as fast as possible, made his escape. The Faraday pouch that contained both his and Sir Andrew's phone was in the car, but concerned about the risk of being tracked he chose to leave them where they were. After driving for around thirty minutes he used a public payphone to raise the alarm at the Met, but gave only limited details and did not say where he intended taking his prisoner. Keen to avoid being caught on any CCTV cameras and as far as possible eliminate the risk of being followed, he travelled only on minor roads and made occasional detours. Despite the apparent randomness of his route he did in fact have a particular destination in mind. It was the only place where he thought it would be safe for him to go.

Day Two - Tuesday

The Reverend Chris Brazelle was in his kitchen at Holford's Cottage having an early breakfast, when a car drove into the yard and he went out to investigate. On seeing a dishevelled, bloodied and roughly bandaged Jenkins he did not need to say a word, the expression on his face spoke for him.

"It's a long story," was all that an unsmiling Jenkins could think of saying in response.

Brazelle gestured for his unexpected visitor to follow him into the cottage and through to the kitchen where he offered him some breakfast. Jenkins gratefully accepted.

After several minutes had passed, during which neither man said a word, Jenkins eventually spoke. "I suppose I should start by telling you that Sir Andrew and five other police officers were killed last night."

With Jenkins' unscheduled early morning arrival, especially given the state he was in, Brazelle anticipated hearing some unpleasant news. He hoped there was no more to come. "I'm very sorry to hear that," he said. His sympathy was sincere and he was keen to learn more, but thought it best to leave Jenkins to explain things in his own good time. Enquiries about his visitor's injuries though, were an entirely different matter. "Would you like me to get someone to come and take a look at your wounds?" he asked.

Jenkins nodded. "Yes. Thanks. I would. But as you'll certainly have guessed, I'm not here on a social visit or a simple courtesy call. You're just about the only person I'm sure I can trust right now. It's important you feel the same about anyone else who gets to know I'm here. Given your history, I'm sure you'll understand exactly what I mean."

Brazelle did indeed understand and he knew exactly who to call. A few minutes later he returned from the study having phoned his good friend Gerald Caulfield, the village doctor.

Over breakfast, Jenkins told Brazelle about the safe-house, described the events of the previous evening and explained the precautions he'd taken to prevent anyone from knowing his current whereabouts.

Brazelle expressed his surprise that there were so few people guarding Gant, given he was such a high value prisoner.

"The Commissioner was concerned that even the Met might have been penetrated by Gant's organisation," Jenkins explained. "He wanted to keep things very tight with only a very limited number of people involved. He was relying on what he called, 'secrecy and seclusion'. It seems his confidence was misplaced. And it was only by chance we were both at the safe-house when it all happened. We weren't due to go over there until later this week, but the Chief made a sudden change of plan."

Brazelle was still a little baffled. "Well, you seem to have covered everything, except for one small detail. Where's Gant?"

The two men went out into the yard where Jenkins opened the boot of his car. Brazelle looked in at the handcuffed

Gant who appeared very different from the last time he had seen him, right down to the look of sheer terror on his face.

"Is any of this legal?" Brazelle asked.

"Doubtful," replied Jenkins, as he pulled his prisoner out of the boot.

Whilst Jenkins parked his car out of site in one of the outbuildings, Brazelle took Gant into his cottage and asked if he'd like to use the bathroom.

Still having in mind the threats that Jenkins had made earlier, Gant chose not to speak. He simply nodded in the affirmative and raised his handcuffed hands to emphasize that he was rather limited with regard to the functions he might be able to perform.

Jenkins was somewhat reluctant to remove his prisoner's handcuffs, even for a few minutes. But Brazelle insisted that he should and, with his hands temporarily freed, Gant disappeared into the bathroom and closed the door.

"Have you seen the size of my bathroom window?" Brazelle asked, rhetorically. "Even a circus contortionist couldn't get through it, let alone a sixteen stoner like Gant. I don't think you need to worry about your prisoner escaping. In any case, where would he go? He now knows that his former associates aren't coming to save him, but planning on permanently silencing him. It's pretty obvious they put a lot of effort into tracking him down and trying to kill him last night. They must believe he has information that's worth keeping secret and see him as a potential weak link, someone who might be persuaded or coerced into revealing it. He's of no further use to them now that his cover is blown, and we already know how utterly ruthless they are. From their point of view the easiest and least risky option is to eliminate him. Sooner or later he must realise that cooperating with you is his best course of action, if he wants a chance of living on into old age. And amoral narcissists like him usually do. In the meantime, though, you'll have your work cut out just keeping him and yourself alive. Maybe I can help you with that."

"Well, I could certainly do with all the help I can get," said Jenkins. "But for the time being, I don't think I can trust anyone at the Met. I'm as certain as I can be that the leak must have come from there. Apart from me and those who died last night, the only other people who knew where we were keeping Gant were Commander Harris and Deputy Commissioner Brompton."

"As far as you know," said Brazelle. "But is it possible someone else knew? Perhaps even someone who isn't a member of the Met?"

Jenkins was doubtful. "I guess it's possible. But it has to be very, very unlikely. All the arrangements were made in face to face conversations. There was no document trail. It was all done strictly off the books and everyone involved understood how sensitive it was. I find it very hard to believe that anyone blabbed, accidentally or otherwise, unless as a deliberate act of treachery. Whilst I was driving here I considered many possibilities, but I kept coming back to the same thought. It has to be either Harris or Brompton who is the traitor."

The discussion would have continued, but the bathroom door opened and Gant exited. He put his hands together and offered up his wrists to Jenkins who immediately re-handcuffed him. Brazelle went into the kitchen, but quickly reappeared with some food and drink which he placed on the table in front of Gant.

Gant had not uttered a word since leaving the farmhouse, but suddenly chose to speak. "His codename is Austin," he said. "The codename of your traitor in the Met is Austin." Although Gant had been in police custody for four weeks and been questioned on numerous occasions this was the first piece of information he had chosen to give.

Jenkins reacted with surprise. "And what do you know about Austin?" he asked.

"I only know that a source of information for our organisation occupies a senior post in the Met and that his codename is Austin," Gant replied. "I know nothing more about him and certainly not his true identity. We only ever refer to individuals in the organisation using codenames and, for some reason of which I am unaware, they are all the names of American towns and cities. My own codename is Detroit, and I believe you gentlemen were acquainted with the late Orlando."

Brazelle was intrigued. "You refer to Austin using the masculine pronoun. How do you know Austin is male? Have you ever seen him? Do you know what he looks like?"

Gant shook his head. "No, I've never met him and I have no idea what he looks like. I have simply assumed that Austin is male because on the one occasion my handler referred to him he used the masculine pronoun. Since my handler was also Austin's handler, I assume he's met him and knows his true identity."

"Why have you decided to volunteer this information now?" asked Brazelle. "And more importantly, are you willing to provide any more?"

Gant gave a faint smile. "Because of my status in the world I share with you, you no doubt think that I have high status in my other world. But you would be wrong. I am but a small cog in a very large and complex machine. My understanding of its motivations and operations, let alone its constituent parts, is extremely limited, but there are some features of which I have knowledge and would be willing to divulge, on a strictly quid pro quo basis. Last night Chief Inspector Jenkins saved my life. What I have told you so far has been in exchange for that favour. Anything else that I give you must be in exchange for something more. I overheard some of your discussion whilst I was in the bathroom. And you are right. After the events of last night I realise that as far as my former associates are concerned I am not just expendable, but a potential risk that must be eliminated. I am of course hoping that you will agree to help me live on into that old age you mentioned, but there is something rather more urgent and pressing that I would be grateful in receiving your help to secure."

"And what is that?" asked Brazelle.

"The safety of my wife," Gant replied. "I've had no contact with her for over four weeks and have no idea how she's coping. But more than that, for those who wish to do me harm, apart from getting to me directly, they may well believe that she is the only other route. If you take me to a place of safety and bring my wife to join me, then I will agree to tell you everything I know."

The potential implications of Gant's proposal were being thought through by Brazelle and Jenkins when Gerald's car pulled into the yard. Brazelle went out to greet him.

Gerald looked Brazelle up and down. "So, what's wrong with you?" he asked. "You look pretty much okay to me?"

When Brazelle had earlier phoned Gerald and asked him to make a professional visit to his home he had not provided him with any further details. As Gerald entered the cottage he was therefore surprised to come across the dishevelled, bloodied and roughly bandaged Jenkins, with his Glock visible in his shoulder holster, and the handcuffed Gant.

Gerald had never encountered Jenkins before and although he had met Gant once, a few weeks previously, given the change of context and the fact that Gant was unshaven, somewhat unkempt and handcuffed, there was no instant recognition.

Brazelle pointed at Jenkins. "This is your patient, Gerald, Chief Inspector Jenkins of the Metropolitan Police Service."

Jenkins smiled and raised his bandaged right hand in a gesture of greeting. A rather nonplussed Gerald returned a faint smile and nodded an acknowledgement.

Brazelle then pointed to the seated and handcuffed Gant. "And this is Sir Ted Gant, former Deputy Director of the Secret Intelligence Service, MI6. He's Rose's godfather and you perhaps remember meeting him at her twenty-fifth birthday party at Harfield House a few weeks ago." Brazelle was referring to his fiancée, the beautiful Rose Harfield. It had been at her home, Harfield House, where Gant had been arrested by Sir Andrew and Jenkins a few weeks earlier, shortly after Rose's twenty-fifth birthday. It was also the occasion when Rose heard for the first time that Gant was the man who, twenty years earlier, had given instructions that her father, Sir Cornelius Harfield, should be killed. Instructions then carried out by Orlando.

Gerald stood in silence and pondered the situation for a few moments, before approaching Jenkins, undoing the roughly applied bandage that was wrapped around his left arm and inspecting the wound. "How did you get this?" he asked.

"I was shot," Jenkins replied.

Gerald then undid the bandage around Jenkins head. "And how did you get this?"

Jenkins winced slightly as Gerald probed his wound. "I hit my head on a wall after being shot."

Finally, Gerald turned his attention to the cut across the palm of Jenkins' right hand. "What about this?"

"I cut myself on a piece of glass when I was climbing into a farmhouse through a broken window."

Gerald gently nodded in a way suggesting he had achieved a degree of insight into the situation in which he had just found himself. "I can't help feeling that I might have just walked in on some form of conspiracy," he said. He waited for a response of some kind, but none came. "I see," he said eventually. "I'll take your collective silence to be confirmation that I'm right. However, the interests of the patient must always come first. And I doubt I can be put in jail for tending to the sick and injured, especially when it's a policeman." He gestured for Jenkins to follow him. "Come into the kitchen and I'll clean up your wounds and take a closer look."

Gant waited until he was alone with Brazelle before speaking again. "I asked Andrew Carpenter about you. He told me nothing, of course, but it's obvious you're no ordinary priest. What are you, ex-military?"

"I'm ex many things," Brazelle replied. "But I prefer to live in the present and look to the future. And, for what it's worth, my advice is that you should do the same. I suggest you cooperate fully, not just to save your own life, but to have any chance of saving your wife's. You, more than anyone, will appreciate the long reach and the ruthlessness of the organisation you've been part of."

Gant nodded. "Indeed I do. And when I was part of it, it was reassuring to know that the organisation could call upon support from just about anywhere. Now, of course, my feeling is quite the opposite. Do you really think that you and Jenkins can protect me and my wife from such a ruthless, all-pervasive and well resourced organisation?"

Brazelle gave a shrug. "Time alone will tell, but I know where we can make a start. Where do you think your wife is most likely to be?"

"After I was arrested she went to stay with her sister on the Isle of Man. Whether or not she's still there, I don't know. As I said, I haven't been allowed any contact with her for over four weeks. I doubt she will have gone home though, because of all the media interest. She's probably been doing her best to keep as low a profile as possible. If you give me a pen and paper I'll write down her sister's details and some other addresses where she might be."

A short while later Gerald and Jenkins, his wounds now re-dressed with clean bandages, returned to the sitting room.

"The wounds are all clean and stitched," said Gerald. "They should all heal up within a couple of weeks or so, but if not, have someone take another look at them. Fortunately, although the bullet wound led to a fair amount of bleeding, the actual trauma it caused is quite limited." He looked at Gant. "While I'm here I might as well give you a quick examination as well."

Brazelle went into the study and made a phone call. By the time he returned to the sitting room Gerald had just finished carrying out Gant's check-up and was giving him some feedback. "You seem to be essentially okay, but your blood pressure is a bit on the high side, which is probably not too surprising given the circumstances you find yourself in. And you could probably do with losing a few pounds."

"Well, where he's likely to be going it will be meagre but healthy rations for a while, so both matters should improve," said Brazelle.

Gerald began to repack his bag. "Is there anything else you need from me, Chris?"

"Just your discretion," Brazelle replied. "I promise to explain everything as soon as I can."

Gerald confirmed his understanding and left.

"Any ideas on what we do next?" asked Jenkins. "I'm afraid I haven't got anything very useful to propose. My plans didn't extend beyond getting here in one piece."

"That's okay," said Brazelle. "I've started a process already."

For some time Jenkins had survived on adrenaline, but the effects had long since begun to wear off and his lack of sleep was starting to become obvious. Brazelle suggested he went into the bedroom and got some rest. He allocated the sofa to Gant, telling him that a very dear friend had slept on it on several occasions and had assured him it was comfortable.

Almost as soon as Jenkins's head touched the pillow he fell into a deep sleep. He would probably have gone on sleeping for much longer, but after about four hours Brazelle woke him. On entering the sitting room he discovered there was a new arrival, but no sign of Gant.

"Gant is quite secure," said Brazelle, reassuringly. "He's being looked after by Max. And I'm sure you remember Major Daniel Coyte-Sherman, my friend from Military Intelligence."

Max had been the senior NCO in the special-forces unit once commanded by Brazelle. The pair had both taken the decision to retire from military service at the same time, a little over five years previously. Their mutual decision was made soon after their involvement in a particularly traumatic military operation, during which five of their comrades, including Coyte-Sherman's twin brother, Martin, had been killed, and they themselves had been seriously wounded. The team had been betrayed and ambushed whilst on a covert military operation in South Africa. Only very recently was it discovered that the person who betrayed them was Ted Gant.

Soon after Brazelle had taken a lease on Holford, a small-holding belonging to the Harfield Estate, Max had become a sub-tenant of his former CO, occupying a self-contained studio flat on the first floor of one of the outbuildings across the yard from his cottage.

Both Max and Daniel Coyte-Sherman had had a part to play in the events that eventually led to Gant's arrest. And it had been Max, with his shotgun, who had brought an end to Orlando's career as an assassin.

Jenkins and Coyte-Sherman had met before, but their previous encounters had not been particularly good tempered events. This explained why, on this occasion, an exchange of acknowledging nods was probably as much as could be hoped for.

Brazelle had called Coyte-Sherman earlier and asked him to come over, but told him very little. Since his arrival he had been fully briefed on the situation and had agreed to help.

"I already have somewhere in mind where we can hold Gant. For a while, at least," said Coyte-Sherman. "I'll need to involve a few members of my unit in Military Intelligence, but they're all used to not asking too many questions and keeping their mouth shut. Chris told me that Gant has agreed to cooperate if we bring his wife to join him." Coyte-Sherman held up a sheet of paper. "He's given us this list of addresses where she might be hiding herself away, so we'll start with these and see if we can find her. Then I'll have a couple of our interrogators get as much information as possible out of Gant. I know he claims not to know much about the organisation he's been part of, but my years of working in Intelligence have taught me that when experienced interrogators get to work, individuals can end up revealing far more than they ever realised they knew."

"And there's one more person we'll have to bring into the picture," said Brazelle, "General Michaels, the Head of the Army. If he ever found out we'd got involved in a matter like this without telling him, we'd all be for the high jump, regardless of the reasons we tried to give him. But after I explain what's happened, he'll understand what's at stake and I'm pretty sure he'll agree with what we're doing. The only real concern I have is that he might decide to tell the Secretary for Defence, or the PM. And I don't know how they'll react. Reading the minds of politicians has never been a strong point of mine. But the General can be very persuasive and he's had a lot of experience dealing with the vanity and anxieties of politicians."

Having been given the outline of the plan, Jenkins gave his reaction. "Well I definitely can't come up with a better proposal. And you guys have access to resources that I certainly don't have. I'm grateful you're both willing to stick your neck out and get involved."

Brazelle smiled. "Good. Then we're agreed. And remember Chief Inspector, Danny and I aren't just getting involved as a favour to you. We're dealing with an organisation that is ultimately responsible for the death of several of our friends, including Danny's twin brother. Not to mention the murder of Rose's father, Sir Cornelius Harfield, and, indirectly, the death of her mother, Justine. That makes it very personal for both of us and also for Max."

After the events of the previous night it had also become personal for Jenkins.

Brazelle pointed to a device that Coyte-Sherman was holding. "I asked Danny to bring along an electronic scanner. I wanted to be certain that you haven't been bugged. We started with your car and you'll be glad to know it's clean. We even scanned Gant – just to be sure. That just leaves you."

Whilst Jenkins was undergoing his scan, Brazelle picked up a large dagger that was lying on the table. "We found this in your car. How do you come to have it?"

"I took it off the first of the attackers I killed and then used it to slit the throat of the second," replied Jenkins.

"Ye gods!" exclaimed Coyte-Sherman. "That must've been a night to remember."

"Or, ideally forget," said Jenkins. "I thought it might prove useful in trying to identify the attackers. It has some script, DINK WEER, etched on the handle. I don't know what it means, but I'm pretty sure it's what I heard the sixth gunman say to Gant, just before I shot him in the head."

"I think my earlier comment was right," said Coyte-Sherman. "It really does sound like a night to remember."

Something Jenkins had said earlier was playing on Brazelle's mind and he decided to return to the subject. "I've been thinking about your theory, your conclusion even, that either Harris or Brompton is a traitor who betrayed the whereabouts of the safe-house. And I have some serious doubts about it. Both men have known about the safe-house from the very beginning, so why leave it all these weeks before carrying out the attack? If the whole point was to silence Gant, then surely they would have wanted to do it as soon as possible. The longer they waited, the more likely it was that he'd give something away. As far as I'm concerned, the timing of the raid strongly suggests that it was only very recently the attackers found out where Gant was being held. Maybe one of the people who knew the location of the safe-house divulged its whereabouts, either carelessly or deliberately, sometime within the last few days, perhaps to someone they thought they could trust."

"Well I can assure you it wasn't me," Jenkins protested, "or the officers stationed at the safe-house. For the past few weeks their only point of contact in the outside world has been the Commissioner himself. And I find it impossible to believe that it was Sir Andrew either. So, even if I'm wrong and you're right, we still come back to it being either Harris or Brompton, although perhaps not acting as a traitor...... just an idiot."

Brazelle smiled. "You really do have it in for the pair of them, don't you? And your confidence in the Commissioner is understandable, but we're all capable of making the occasional error of judgement. And that includes even him. But leaving such thoughts aside for the moment, there is still one more possibility. Don't you think it's a bit of a coincidence that the attack took place such a very short time after you and Sir Andrew arrived at the safe-house? I don't know how you normally react to coincidences, but they frequently leave me with something of an uneasy feeling. Especially coincidences like this one. It's got me wondering if, despite all the precautions you took and our failure to find any evidence of it, somehow, you really were tracked to the safe-house yesterday. I'm definitely going to keep that possibility in mind. For the time being though, I think we should concentrate on looking for any evidence that someone leaked the information. And I suggest we start with Sir Andrew. Do you know what kind of security is on his phone?"

"Just a password, I believe," Jenkins replied. "Although I don't know what it is. Why do you want to know?"

"Because his phone might help us identify who he had contact with over the past few days," Brazelle replied. "However unlikely it may seem, it's still possible that Sir Andrew recently told someone about the safe-house. It may have been a deliberate act, or perhaps it was done carelessly. In any case, it's all we've got to go on at the moment. And we have to start somewhere."

Sir Andrew's phone was lying on the table with its battery removed. Coyte-Sherman picked it up and gave a shrug. "Not knowing the phone's password won't be a problem. We have people who can access just about anything."

"And when they do, check out the last few days and let us know if you find anything of interest," Brazelle instructed.

Coyte-Sherman gave a nod. "Understood. Anything else?"

"Yes. How long can you give to this, Danny?" Brazelle asked. "Exactly how long do you think we've got?"

"I'd say a week; maybe; if we're lucky," Coyte-Sherman replied. "That's before my CO starts asking me to explain what I've been doing with my time. But you know how we work in Military Intelligence, Chris. The impossible we do immediately, although the miraculous might take a bit longer. I'll be in touch as soon as I have anything to report."

By the time Coyte-Sherman left with Gant it was past noon and Brazelle thought he should carry out at least a few professional tasks that day. Leaving Jenkins at Holford's Cottage, he went to St Catherine's, the Prinsted village church, where he was the acting parish priest during the absence on maternity leave of the regular incumbent, Reverend Jenny Caulfield, Gerald's wife. Whilst he was there he sent a one word coded message to General Michaels. He soon received the briefest of replies: 'PPT12'.

It was early evening by the time Brazelle returned home to Holford's Cottage and made a start on preparing some supper for himself and his house guest. "Is there any food that you're allergic to, Ifor?" he asked.

"Only to the lack of it," Jenkins replied.

Over supper Jenkins explained his plans for the immediate future. "Now that Gant's taken care of I'll head back to London in the morning. Deputy Commissioner Brompton will now be in charge, so I'll have to see him first. But I'm not going to tell him where I've been or what I've been doing since leaving the safe-house. And I certainly won't be mentioning you or what we've done with Gant."

"So, what exactly will you tell him?" asked Brazelle.

Jenkins gave a faint shrug. "At the moment I have no idea. I'll have to make it up as I go along, I guess, just like I did last night. But this time without all the dead bodies, hopefully!" Keen to change the subject he pointed to a painting of St Catherine's Church that was hanging on the sitting room wall. "I seem to remember this picture was standing on your easel, still needing to be finished, the last time I was here."

Brazelle was impressed. "That was over four weeks ago and you were only here for a matter of minutes. You must have very sharp powers of observation, and a good memory. I got it finished a few days after you last saw it."

There was a new canvas now standing on Brazelle's easel. He removed the cloth covering it to reveal a nearly-finished portrait of his fiancée, Rose Harfield. "This is my current work in progress, and it's a bit of a departure from my usual efforts. I'm more of an architecture or landscape painter, rather than a portrait artist. But I thought I'd try something different. I did quite a bit of research on the history and techniques of portrait painting before I started on the project. It was all fascinating stuff."

It was now Jenkins' turn to be impressed. "I know nothing about art, but I can recognise skill and talent when I see it. And I can see it in this portrait of Rose. Has she seen it yet?"

Brazelle shook his head. "No. And as far as I'm aware she knows nothing about it. She's aware I did a couple of sketches of her and took a few photographs a couple of weeks back, but I didn't tell her I've been using them as the basis of a portrait. I didn't want her to know about it until it's finished. That's why I keep it covered up, although she's hardly likely to see it at the moment. She's in the States sorting out the sale of a business she owns over there. I was hoping to get it finished by the time she gets back, but given what I've now got involved in I guess it's going to take a bit longer than I'd planned."

"What sort of business does she own?" asked Jenkins.

"It's a martial arts school in Manhattan called The Vixen School of Self Defence and Focussed Agression. And they only train females."

Jenkins was surprised. "Martial arts? Does she do any of that stuff herself?"

"A little," Brazelle replied, with deep understatement, as he remembered the Sunday lunchtime in the village tavern a few weeks earlier, when Rose inflicted painful and humiliating punishment on three fit young men. For a moment, the memory of it made him smile, but his smile disappeared as he recalled the premeditation and almost cold-blooded ruthlessness with which she had acted, and the slight feeling of unease it had induced in him at the time.

Day Three - Wednesday

In the hours since Jenkins reported the attack on the safe-house and the death of Sir Andrew and the other police officers, the news had spread rapidly throughout the Met and beyond. It was inevitable that his arrival at New Scotland Yard would not be a low key affair, especially since he turned up wrapped in bandages. Keen to minimise the fuss, he made his way to the Commissioner's office as quickly as possible via the shortest possible route. Deputy Commissioner Brompton was now Acting Commissioner and Jenkins assumed he would have already installed himself in Sir Andrew's office. His assumption was correct.

Having not been given any pre-warning of Jenkins' arrival, Grace McAllister was taken by surprise. "I'm so glad to see you Chief Inspector," she said. "We've all been ever so worried about you, especially not having heard anything from you since that first phone call you made. And I can't tell you how shocked and saddened I was when I heard what had happened to Sir Andrew and the others. As you can imagine, it's been absolute bedlam here. I've never known it like this in all the years I've worked here. DC Brompton's already moved into the Commissioner's office. I'll let him know you're here. I'm sure he'll want to see you straightaway."

Mrs. McAllister was right. Just seconds later Jenkins was in the Commissioner's office, standing to attention in front of DC Brompton.

"I'm glad to see you, Chief Inspector," said Brompton, before making vague hand gestures towards Jenkins's bandages. "Are any of your injuries serious? Have they been looked at?"

Jenkins guessed he'd just been asked the two easiest questions that were heading his way. "No, none of them is serious. And, yes, they've been looked at already, thank you, Sir," he replied.

Brompton gave a faint nod and gestured for Jenkins to sit down. "Good, I'm glad about that. When you didn't turn up after your phone-call alerting us to what had happened we were naturally concerned about you, but we'll come to that later. I've asked Commander Harris to join us. As you will appreciate Jenkins, this is an incredibly sensitive situation we find ourselves in. There are many questions to be asked and you appear to be the only person who can answer them."

Once Commander Harris entered the room the questioning began.

"First off, where's Gant?" asked Brompton.

Jenkins gave an honest reply. "I don't know, Sir."

"Don't know!" exclaimed Brompton. "Has he escaped?"

Jenkins shook his head. "No, Sir, he hasn't escaped. I have every reason to believe he's quite secure."

Brompton, who had a reputation for having a short fuse, began to redden in the face. "You say you don't know where he is, but that he's quite secure. How do you know? Who has custody of him?"

Jenkins knew he was about to tread blindfold into a minefield and swallowed hard before giving his reply. "I'm afraid I'm not at liberty to say, Sir."

Brompton looked like he might have a seizure at any moment, but the much calmer and seemingly restrained Commander Harris stepped in. "May I ask a few questions of the Chief Inspector, Sir?" he asked.

Brompton, looking exasperated, said nothing, but gestured with his hand for Harris to take over and sat back in his chair.

Harris' style was much less aggressive and emotional. "Let's take a step back and start again shall we?" he proposed. "In the phone call you made to the Emergency Response Unit, you said that the safe-house where Gant was being held had been attacked by a group of heavily armed men and that you had killed six of them. However, very sadly, all of your six colleagues, including Sir Andrew, had also been killed during the attack. Eventually, not knowing whether or not there were any more gunmen around, but thinking you had a reasonable chance of escape, you managed to get to your car and leave the scene, taking Gant with you. Apart from providing the precise location of the safe-house and giving my name as the point of contact for details of the contingency plan to be put into operation, the only other details you gave concerned the disposition of the dead bodies. You said there were twelve bodies in total, ten inside the safe-house, including the six police officers, and two more outside. Have I left anything out, Jenkins?"

Jenkins shook his head. "No, I don't think you've left anything out, Sir. I deliberately kept the call as brief as possible because, at that point, I couldn't be sure whether or not I was being followed."

"I think the Deputy Commissioner and I both completely understand your actions at that time," said Harris. "However the situation is quite different now and it is essential that you provide a lot more detail than you have done so far. But before you do, I shall tell YOU a few things. Immediately after we received your phone call, a SWAT team and a Crime Scene Investigation Unit were sent to the safe-house. On arrival they found the building ablaze, but no sign or evidence of any attackers, either dead or alive. Once the fire was extinguished and it was possible to enter the building and carry out a search, the remains of only six bodies were discovered. Although their identities have yet to be formally confirmed, it's quite clear that they are the bodies of the six police officers who we know were at the safe-house, including, of course, Sir Andrew. The next of kin of the officers have been informed, which is just as well, since speculation regarding their identities is circulating on social media and Sir Andrew's death is already being reported in the mainstream media." Harris paused for a moment allowing Jenkins to give his reaction to what he'd just been told.

"I can only assume that sometime after I got away with Gant, associates of the attackers removed their bodies, before setting the building on fire. I really can't think of any other explanation."

"Tell him the rest of it, Commander," said Brompton, brusquely.

Harris continued. "The only weapon that was found undamaged by the fire was a sniper rifle. It was discovered lying on the ground about forty yards in front of the farmhouse. And guess what?"

Before Harris could answer his own question, Jenkins answered it for him. "My fingerprints were all over it."

"Yes, that's right," said Harris, "yours and nobody elses. So I'm sure you can guess what my next question is. How did they get there?"

"The rifle belonged to the second attacker that I killed," said Jenkins. "He'd used it to shoot Dorrian and Forbes, before we even knew we were under attack. After I'd killed him I used it to shoot two more of the gunmen, before leaving it where I found it. Only my fingerprints were found on the weapon because the sniper, just like all of his five associates, was wearing gloves."

Harris took several minutes to scribble in his note-book before speaking again. "Because of the potentially dangerous nature of the operation, all of the police officers in the safe house were armed, weren't they?"

Jenkins nodded. "Yes, everyone was armed with a Glock and a Heckler and Koch G36, except for the Commissioner and me. We only had Glocks."

"And where is your weapon now?" asked Harris.

"I handed it in, together with all the remaining ammunition as soon as I arrived here. In accordance with regulations," Jenkins replied.

DC Brompton leaned forward and pressed the switch on his intercom. "Grace, have someone collect the weapon and ammunition that Chief Inspector Jenkins returned when he arrived in the building. And then have them taken over to forensics."

Brompton switched off the intercom, sat back in his chair once more and gestured for Harris to continue. "So far the remains of several dozen spent shells and bullets have been recovered from inside the farmhouse, but the search is ongoing so more may yet be found. Regrettably, however, with the sole exception of the bullets that killed Dorrian and Forbes, because of impact damage and the effects of the fire, they think it's unlikely they'll be able to connect many of the bullets back to a specific weapon. But do you know the oddest thing, Jenkins?"

Harris' question was meant to be rhetorical, but Jenkins nevertheless gave an answer. "They think they might all have come from either a Glock or a G36."

Harris nodded. "Yes, that's right, except for the bullets that killed Dorrian and Forbes, which it seems were almost certainly fired from the sniper rifle that carries your fingerprints. All very puzzling, don't you think?"

"No, I don't think it's puzzling at all, Sir," replied Jenkins. "Apart from the sniper rifle, all of the attackers were carrying the same weaponry as me and the other police officers: Glocks and G36s. And what's more they were wearing standard Met issue body armour and carrying Met issue radios. In fact, since they were all wearing similar dark clothing, in the twilight, they were almost indistinguishable from a Met SWAT team."

DC Brompton, who had been listening in silence, suddenly interrupted. "Let's get this straight Jenkins. Are you suggesting that the safe-house was attacked by a police SWAT team?"

Jenkins shook his head. "No, Sir, I'm just saying that the attackers were kitted out identically to a SWAT team. I searched three of the bodies, but found absolutely nothing to give a clue to their identity. And, apart from the sniper rifle, the only item I came across that wasn't standard Met issue was a dagger that one of them was carrying."

"And where's that dagger now?" asked Harris.

"I'm afraid I'm not at liberty to say, Sir," Jenkins replied.

"Oh, so we're back to that now, are we, Jenkins?" said a furious DC Brompton. "So just what are you at liberty to say, before I tell you what I think?"

Jenkins chose his words carefully. "The attackers didn't come to rescue Gant. They came to kill him. And he knows it. Because of that, he's agreed to cooperate and tell what he knows about the organisation he was working for. And I've taken steps to secure his safety while he does. Only the Met was involved with Gant's security, so it seems to me that there must be a traitor somewhere amongst us who divulged Gant's whereabouts. As far as I'm aware, the only people who knew where Gant was being held were the six officers who are dead and the three people in this room. For that reason I think it best, at least for the time being, that I say nothing that might give a clue to where Gant is currently being held. I'm hoping that you will understand and agree."

Brompton was far from being appeased. "You've presumably thought through all the implications of what you've just said, Jenkins. You're suggesting that the supposed traitor who might have divulged Gant's whereabouts is either me, or Commander Harris. But then there are the implications for you. Until Gant is once more in police custody he must be considered a fugitive from justice. And through your refusal to give him up you are committing the very serious crime of aiding and abetting him. However, before we pursue that matter, let me give you my reading of the evidence, Chief Inspector. We have six dead police officers, two killed by a sniper rifle that carries only your fingerprints, and four killed by a weapon of a type to which you are known to have had access. Unfortunately, a great deal of potential forensic evidence was destroyed in the fire, presumably deliberately, including by the way, any recorded evidence that might have been caught on CCTV. And finally, and perhaps most compelling of all, you refuse to hand over Gant. I don't think you need to be a genius to see what I might be thinking, Jenkins."

"And I can only agree," said Harris. "It seems to me that the only way for you to remove the suspicions that the Deputy Commissioner and I may have, is to tell us what you've done with Gant. You will also be removing the immediate threat of being charged with aiding and abetting a fugitive."

In what he said next, Brompton adopted a more conciliatory tone. "In my entire police career, thank God, I have never had the need to fire a gun at another human being. Whereas, if what you say is true, then in just one evening you found it necessary to kill six men. I cannot begin to imagine the impact that such an experience had on you, but I can certainly believe it may have temporarily warped your judgement. With that in mind, I am going to allow you a little more time to reflect on the attitude that you have so far adopted. You have precisely one hour, Chief Inspector, to come to your senses and tell us what you've done with Gant, or, at the very least, I shall arrest you and charge you with aiding and abetting a fugitive. Am I sufficiently clear?"

"Yes, Sir, totally clear," Jenkins replied.

Brompton instructed Jenkins to go straight to his office and remain there for exactly one hour. He was then to return and answer all the questions that were put to him, or face arrest.

Jenkins went to leave, but on reaching the office door suddenly stopped and turned back to face Brompton. "May I ask you both a question, Sir?"

"Yes, very well. What is it?" snapped Brompton.

"Does the name Austin mean anything to either of you?"

Brompton took on a quizzical look. "That's a very strange question."

"I agree," said Harris. "But, since you ask, the only thing that comes to my mind is a car. My father had an Austin. But they stopped making them years ago. Why on earth do you ask?"

Jenkins was deliberately slow in making his reply. "Gant said that his organisation has a source in the Met at a very senior level and that his codename is Austin."

"Did Gant say anything else about this alleged source in the Met?" asked Brompton.

"I'm afraid I'm not at liberty to say, Sir," replied Jenkins, before quickly leaving the room, closing the door behind him.

Commander Harris returned to the Commissioner's office exactly one hour after the first interview of Jenkins had ended, only to be told that Jenkins had absconded.

"It appears that the bird has flown," said DC Brompton. "I've just learned that Jenkins exited the building very soon after he left this office. I feel a damn fool for not having put him under some form of supervision."

"Maybe we've read the whole thing wrong so far, Sir," said Harris. "I've been thinking through everything Jenkins told us and, to be honest, I find it really quite plausible. In fact, I find it far easier to believe than any alternative that comes to mind. If he was telling the truth then he wouldn't have anticipated any problem having us believe him. The bodies of the gunmen, their weapons and kit, and any CCTV recordings that existed, would all have backed up his story. And, of course, he was right about those who had knowledge of the safe-house. As far as he or either of us knows, we are the only surviving people who knew about it. Given Gant's alleged claim that there is a traitor occupying a senior position here at the Met, Jenkins's decision not to reveal Gant's whereabouts can be seen as wholly rational. To be honest, if I was in his position, I'd probably do the same. And now, when he finds that nobody appears to believe him, he decides to abscond. If he's innocent, then from his point of view it's yet another wholly rational decision to make. On the other hand, if he really is guilty, then surely he could have come up with a better story. The truth is, Sir, I find it really difficult to believe that Jenkins is a guilty man."

DC Brompton was unconvinced. "Just stop for a minute and think through the full implications of your theory,

Harris. If you are right and Jenkins is telling the truth, we must conclude that either you or I divulged the location of the safe-house. Since I know it wasn't me, I would have to assume it's you."

"Not necessarily, Sir," Harris objected. "Perhaps the Commissioner took someone else into his confidence about the location of the safe-house, but chose not to tell us."

Brompton shook his head. "I doubt that very much. What possible reason was there for him to have done that? And the Commissioner kept stressing the importance of saying nothing to anyone else. Not to anyone at all. Whilst I haven't entirely closed my mind to any other possibility, we must go where the evidence leads us. For the moment that suggests we give the highest priority to apprehending Jenkins. However, I don't think we should publicly name him as a person of interest just yet. Nor do I intend to make public the fact that we've lost track of Gant. The time for that may come, but it hasn't arrived yet."

Brazelle drove to Ruislip, parked his jeep and took the Central Line to Lancaster Gate. From there he walked to Kensington Gardens, sat on a bench opposite Peter Pan's statue and opened up his newspaper. At exactly 12 noon, a tall man in his late fifties, wearing a long black gabardine mackintosh and a similarly coloured trilby, came up and spoke to him. "I've just spent two hours listening to a couple of twelve year old politicians tell me how to run the Army, so I could do with a walk in the fresh air. Care to join me?"

"Thanks for agreeing to meet with me, Sir," said Brazelle, as the pair began their stroll around the Gardens. "There's something important you should know and I thought it was best explained face to face."

"I believe I know what you were planning on telling me," said General Michaels. "I've already heard it from Daniel Coyte-Sherman. I sent for him yesterday, just after I received your message asking for an urgent meeting. Knowing the two of you are as thick as thieves, I guessed he'd probably be somehow involved in whatever you'd got yourself into. And it seems I was right. It would appear that the favour I did you a few weeks ago, when I persuaded Andrew Carpenter to meet with you, has had some unanticipated and very serious consequences."

"Did Danny tell you where he's holding Gant?" queried Brazelle.

"No, he didn't. And in the interests of plausible deniability I told him I didn't want to know. If any of this gets out, I want to be as sure of what I don't and never did know, as I am of what I do. And don't get the wrong idea, Chris.

Don't let my apparent quiet acceptance of the situation lead you to think that I actually approve of what you're doing. The best I can stretch to is, tolerate. That's what I've told Daniel and it's what I'm telling you. And bear in mind that if you come unstuck, I won't be able to help you. I've told Daniel to keep me informed, strictly off the record of course. And one more thing, Chris, don't forget that the usual rules of military engagement will apply: if things go wrong you'll both be shot, although these days only metaphorically speaking; but, if it's a success, then the politicians will take all the credit."

"Do you know very much of the background to all this, General?" Brazelle asked. "Did Sir Andrew tell you what he and I discussed at our first meeting?"

"I have no way of knowing if he told me everything," the General replied, "but just over a week after you had your meeting he called to thank me for helping set it up. He said it was only because of my intervention on your behalf that he'd agreed to meet with you, but, afterwards, he was very glad that he did."

"And did he also persuade you to get involved in some way yourself, Sir?" Brazelle asked.

The General made no attempt to answer the question, but stopped walking and put out his hand. "I'm going to have to leave you here, Chris. I'm having lunch with a couple more miniature Napoleons. Good luck!"

General Michaels had near perfect hearing. If he failed to answer a question, Brazelle knew it wouldn't be because he hadn't heard it, but because he chose to ignore it.

The two men shook hands and the General turned to walk away, but after taking only a few paces he paused momentarily. "Tell Max not to worry about his shotgun," he said. "He'll get it back."

Brazelle smiled to himself as he watched the General disappear. Although it had been given indirectly, he had just received an answer to his question. And it was a very clear 'yes'.

It was a dry sunny day and Brazelle was considering wandering around Kensington Gardens for a little while longer when his mobile rang. It was a number he didn't recognise.

Brazelle got off the tube at West Ruislip. As he walked through the car park he was followed at a distance by a tall hooded figure carrying a backpack. On arriving at his jeep both he and the hooded figure got in.

"How confident are you that you weren't followed?" asked Brazelle.

"Very," replied Jenkins. "I'm fast becoming an expert in guile and evasion."

On the way back to Prinsted Jenkins explained what had happened earlier at New Scotland Yard and why he'd taken the decision to abscond. "I didn't see how I had any other option. I couldn't tell them where Gant was, so I would have been held in custody. I don't know how long I'll be AWOL, so I swung by my flat and grabbed a few things before ringing you from a payphone. Thanks for agreeing to pick me up."

Brazelle understood the increased risk. "So from now on it won't be just Gant's former associates who'll want to find you. What do you think the chances are that the police will come looking for you in Prinsted?"

"Very slim, I'd say," said Jenkins. "The Commissioner judged that the evidence we gathered against Gant through our wider investigations was enough to ensure he got put away for the rest of his life. So he focussed exclusively on those matters. In his official report he made no reference to you, the Harfield family, or Prinsted."

Despite Jenkins's attempt at reassurance, Brazelle still needed to be convinced. "What about the two fake policemen who paid me a visit?" he asked. "And what about Orlando, the assassin who came to kill me but instead ended up getting blasted by Max, all over my home?"

"Not a problem," said Jenkins reassuringly. "Both events were dealt with as entirely separate and unrelated matters. The fake policemen settled for a deal. In exchange for pleading guilty to impersonating police officers and being in illegal possession of unlicensed firearms, they avoided being charged with conspiracy to murder and were each given a relatively lenient sentence. They understood, though, that if they ever blabbed about their involvement with Orlando, the conspiracy charge would be reinstated and they'd probably end up getting at least twenty years. And for good measure there was a veiled threat of the 'we know where you live' type. Once they'd accepted the deal, there was no need for witnesses to be called and their case was dealt with in record time. It was all over in a day. You probably know better than me how these things work, Chris. Through certain channels, the prosecuting counsel and the judge were informed there was a matter of national security involved and that both men had supplied valuable information that was helpful to the state. In truth, neither of them had provided anything that was remotely useful, because they weren't established members of Gant's organisation. They were just low-grade freelancers who'd been hired in to carry out a single job and knew even less about what they'd got themselves into than we did."

"And what about Orlando's death?" asked Brazelle. "From beginning to end the whole matter was dealt with very differently to the way I expected. One minute there was the body of a would-be assassin who'd met with a violent death lying in my home, and the next it was gone. Then, within less than twenty four hours and without me having to lift a finger, I had a new bedroom door and carpet fitted, and my cottage had never looked quite so clean and tidy. What's more, neither Max nor I was ever interviewed or asked to give a statement. And nobody has mentioned the matter since. Apart from Max having his shotgun taken off him it's almost as if nothing ever happened."

Jenkins smiled. "I take it you're not unhappy about any of that. I imagine the last thing you or Max would want would be for either of you to become publicly involved." Jenkins knew that both Brazelle and Max had strong reasons for wanting to lead quiet, private lives.

"That's perfectly true," said Brazelle, "but it doesn't mean I'm not curious about how and why things have ended up the way they have."

"Well, there had to be an inquest into Orlando's death, of course," responded Jenkins, "but it was done without any great fuss. I attended it myself, but only as an ordinary member of the public, not in any official capacity. The coroner concluded that Orlando had killed himself with a shotgun, either deliberately or accidentally, but with nobody else involved. For the purpose of the inquest, Orlando had been given a fictitious name and there was no reference to any connection with Gant, Prinsted, or to you or Max."

"And, let me guess," said Brazelle. "The coroner was provided with information through those 'certain channels' you referred to earlier."

Again Jenkins smiled. "As you well know Chris, nothing is impossible when the higher powers see something as a potential source of political embarrassment, especially if it can be covered up and made to go away by claiming it to be a matter of national security."

"And whose idea was all this? Was it the Commissioner's?" Brazelle asked.

"Originally, yes," replied Jenkins. "But it wasn't too difficult to get the politicians to go along with it. I don't know how he arranged to get your place cleaned up and all the evidence linking you and Max to Orlando's death removed, though. He played his cards very close to his chest with that one and said it was best I knew as little as possible, just in case it ever hit the fan. If that did happen then I could, in all honesty, say I knew nothing about it. I don't think he even told the PM the whole story, but there was one other person he must have told. He never mentioned a name, just said there was someone who owed him a favour. I assume that was the person who arranged for the clean-up of your place."

Brazelle thought he might know who that 'someone' was, but still had questions on another matter. "From what you say, it seems highly unlikely that anyone reading Sir Andrew's report would make much of a connection between you and me, or Prinsted. But you said it was his 'official' report. Is there an unofficial version?"

Jenkins hesitated before giving his answer. "Yes, there is. The official report was going to form the basis of the case against Gant and used to prosecute him, but the Chief also created a single copy of an unofficial report. It was essentially his official report, but with one extra chapter added. He intended to show it just to the PM and the Home Secretary, but whether or not he'd done that before he was killed, I don't know. Because I was the only other person who knew the whole story, he asked me to take a look through and check it. It's possible I'm the only other person who's ever seen it, or even knows that it exists."

"And what's in this extra chapter?" Brazelle asked.

Jenkins again hesitated before giving his reply. "Just about everything," he said eventually. "It starts from when you unexpectedly turned up in his office and he was pursuaded to see you by General Michaels. And it ends with Gant's arrest at Harfield House. He wrote very little about you, though, and certainly didn't mention your real identity. But anyone reading it would quickly realise you're not exactly a typical priest and must have played a fairly significant role in solving the case."

Brazelle understood the seriousness of what he'd just heard and gave out a sigh. "And where is it now, this unofficial report?"

Jenkins shook his head. "I don't know. But I'm fairly sure it isn't at Scotland Yard. The Chief took it with him when he left the office last Friday, but he didn't have it when he returned on Monday morning. He told me he'd had another look through it over the weekend to check on any amendments I'd suggested and then lodged it somewhere safe."

"Do you know where he went at the weekend?" asked Brazelle.

Jenkins again shook his head. "No, I don't. But I doubt he went home. It had been a particularly busy week and he told me he intended taking the weekend off. When he left the office late on Friday afternoon he'd already changed out of his uniform and into civilian clothes. That was usually a sign he was going straight off somewhere. When he arrived back at the office early on Monday morning he was still dressed in civvies, so it seems highly likely he'd come straight back from wherever he'd spent the weekend."

"I know nothing about Sir Andrew's private life," said Brazelle. "Was he married? Or was there some other significant person in his life who might have been with him over the weekend? Perhaps someone he trusted enough to give his unofficial report to, for safe keeping?"

"I don't know much about his private life either," Jenkins replied. "Sir Andrew was usually very open with me on professional matters because we worked closely together on so many cases, but he was very discreet about personal matters. All I know is that he had been married, but his wife died about five years ago."

Not long after arriving back home, Brazelle received an email from Coyte-Sherman. His team had succeeded in accessing the contents of Sir Andrew's phone and he'd sent copies of two photographs that had been found. The first showed Sir Andrew with his arm around a woman of similar age, as they stood side-by-side with their backs to the sea, somewhere on the coast. The second had the couple sitting in a restaurant sharing a bottle of champagne, with what looked like a birthday cake on the table in front of them. Time stamps on the photographs confirmed they'd been taken within an hour of each other on the previous Saturday. Jenkins immediately recognised the colourful tie that Sir Andrew was wearing in both photographs. It was the same tie he was wearing when he returned to his office on the Monday morning that followed.

"Do you recognise the woman?" asked Brazelle.

Jenkins studied the two photographs. "No. I'm sure I've never seen her before. I have no idea who she is. Have you checked the geo-tagging to find out where they were taken?"

"No. It looks like he had it switched off," Brazelle replied, "but, regardless, I can still tell that the first photograph was taken in Eastbourne. And since the second was taken not much later, I'd guess that it was as well."

"How can you be so sure it was Eastbourne?" asked a skeptical Jenkins.

Brazelle responded with his own question. "Have you ever heard of a man called Eugenius Birch?"

Jenkins shook his head. "Should I have done?"

"Not necessarily," replied Brazelle, as he reached onto his bookshelf and took down a volume entitled: 'Unsung Architectural Heroes of the Victorian Age'. "Eugenius Birch was a seaside architect who specialised in designing piers in coastal resorts during their heyday in the nineteenth century. Most of the more famous ones that still survive were designed by him. I've taken an interest in all types of architecture over the years and come across several examples of his work. They've never failed to impress me and I guess he's become something of a hero of mine."

Brazelle thumbed his way through the book until he found the page with the picture he was searching for and handed it to Jenkins. "Birch designed Eastbourne pier in the eighteen sixties and this is what it looks like these days. Take a good look at it and then look again at the photograph of Sir Andrew and the woman with the sea behind them."

Jenkins compared the two pictures and quickly realised that a small stretch of Eastbourne pier was visible in the background of the photograph.

In the second photograph, obviously taken in a restaurant, it was just possible to make out the mirror reflection of an illuminated sign. It was the lateral inversion of 'Leonardo's'.

"These photographs should help us answer a couple of burning questions," said Brazelle. "It's clear that Sir Andrew spent a good deal of his time with the woman in the photograph during the days immediately prior to the attack on the safe-house. Since he told you on Monday that he'd lodged his unofficial report somewhere safe over the weekend, we should definitely consider the possibility that he left it with her. And if he did trust her enough for that purpose, then what else did he trust her with? I think we ought to find out who she is. Don't you, Ifor?"

Day Four - Thursday

Leonardo's is as far removed from Lillian's Fine Dining as it is possible to imagine. There is certainly no greasy Full English Breakfast on the menu here.

It was a few minutes past noon and the restaurant had just opened ready to begin its lunch time service when Jenkins entered and asked to speak to the manager. A few moments later, a well fed man in his late middle age arrived. He was wearing an ill-fitting suit and a cheap toupée. Jenkins thought his appearance was making a very clear statement: I eat too much, I have very poor dress sense...and I am bald. The man introduced himself as Leonardo, the restaurant's proprietor.

Jenkins showed his police ID and then the photograph of Sir Andrew and the unknown woman sitting at the restaurant table. "Do you recognise the couple in this photograph?" he asked.

Leonardo put on a broad smile. "Yes, of course. I took that photograph myself last Saturday evening at the couple's request. The lady had booked a table and ordered a birthday cake in advance, as a surprise for her friend. When we brought out the cake the staff sang Happy Birthday and most of the other patrons joined in. I think her friend enjoyed it all very much."

"I'm sure he did," said Jenkins with obvious impatience. "But do you know who they are?"

"Well I don't know the gentleman," Leonardo replied, having dropped his smile in response to Jenkins' abruptness. "But I know the lady. She comes here for lunch on her own from time to time."

"What's her name?" Jenkins asked, his impatience clearly growing.

"Julie," replied Leonardo, becoming ever more edgy. "Her name is Julie."

Jenkins' impatience tipped into out-and-out rudeness. "Julie what?" he snapped.

Leonardo began to show signs of mild panic. "I'm sorry officer. I don't know her surname. I only know her as Julie."

Jenkins decided he had to get a grip on himself and eased his tone. "Can you tell me anything else about her? Like where she lives or where she works? And what about your staff, are they likely to know anything?"

Having assured Jenkins he couldn't tell him anything more, Leonardo showed the photograph to his staff, but they could add nothing further.

A disappointed Jenkins retrieved the photograph, thanked the restaurateur for his time and was almost out of the door, when Leonardo called after him. "I have her telephone number, of course."

A slim, attractive woman in her early fifties opened the door of the small detached cottage and invited Jenkins to enter. A few minutes later they were sitting in the lounge, drinking tea.

"I wasn't surprised when you phoned," said Julie. "After I heard on the news that Andrew had been killed, I thought it was only a matter of time before I got a call from the police. We were very discreet about our relationship, but I guessed there would be clues that would lead you to me eventually."

"I'm sorry you had to find out by hearing it on the news," said Jenkins. "It must have come as a terrible shock."

Julie nodded. "Yes, it certainly did. It was not much more than twenty four hours since he'd left here and the last time I saw him. He stayed here over the weekend."

Jenkins was unsure of the best way to phrase his next question but decided that a direct approach was probably the one to take. "I know this will be a difficult time for you, but would you mind if I asked a few questions about your relationship with Sir Andrew?"

Julie gave a faint smile. "Well I guessed you hadn't come to just offer sympathy and drink tea. What would you like to know?"

"Perhaps you could start by telling me when and how the two of you met."

Julie pointed to some flowers that stood in a vase on the table. "Those arrived yesterday, only a few hours before I heard the terrible news. They were sent by Andrew as a sort of anniversary gift. It was exactly one year ago yesterday that we first met. We just happened to be sitting on the same bench on the sea front and struck up a conversation, the way that strangers sometimes do. Things just developed from there. He told me he came down here on occasional weekends, just to relax and take the sea air. I had no idea who he was when we first met. And it wasn't until our third meeting that he told me. I'd seen him on TV a few times, of course, but he'd always been in uniform, looking extremely formal and serious. When I met him down here everything was so very different and I never made the connection. It's amazing how you can sometimes fail to recognise someone if the context in which you see them is changed. I moved here from Abingdon in Oxfordshire, almost three years ago. I was pretty much penniless at the time, but I managed to find a job and a cheap place to rent. About a year later my divorce was finalised and I had enough from the settlement to buy this place. Until meeting Andrew, I hadn't had any kind of close relationship with anyone in all that time. I felt so blessed to have met him. He was widowed and I was divorced, so we certainly weren't doing anything wrong, but I had my reasons for wanting to keep our relationship private. Andrew was happy to go along with that, at least for the first few months, but as our relationship developed he grew much keener to go public. He wanted to introduce me to some of his friends, but I was still rather hesitant. This last weekend rather brought things to a head though. He proposed marriage. And I accepted." She held out her left hand to show an engagement ring she was wearing.

Jenkins was taken completely by surprise, but eventually found some words with which to respond. "I'm really so dreadfully sorry. I had absolutely no idea."

"You mustn't feel embarrassed." Julie assured him. "Andrew promised not to tell anyone about our relationship and I've never doubted that he kept his word. I'm sure you didn't even know of my existence, let alone know how serious our relationship was."

Jenkins paused a moment before continuing. "I was wondering if the Commissioner ever talked about his work,"

"Not really," Julie replied. "When he was with me I think he wanted to stay as far away from his professional life as he possibly could."

"So he never talked to you about Sir Ted Gant?"

"Good heavens no," insisted Julie. "He never discussed any of his cases with me in any sort of detail. He only ever made very general references, usually when he was apologising for having to answer his phone on a work related call, or being called away unexpectedly at short notice, which unfortunately happened once or twice. But he did mention you a couple of times. He obviously thought very highly of you and said you were his officer of choice for any particularly 'sensitive job', as he put it. That's why I knew who you were when you phoned and introduced yourself earlier. You were obviously someone he trusted, so I've assumed I can do the same."

Jenkins unzipped a thin document case, took out two photographs and handed them to Julie. After explaining how he came to have them and that he might never have found her without them, he made a confession. "I think you should know I'm not here officially. No other police officer has ever seen those photographs. In fact, as far as I'm aware, no other police officer knows who you are, or is even aware of your existence. And I won't be telling anyone, unless you want me to."

Julie shook her head. "No, I don't want you to tell anyone. The last thing I want is to be reading about myself in the newspapers. If my identity gets out, then I'm sure that's the least that will happen. But tell me what happened to Andrew. There were almost no details given in the news. They just said that he'd been shot and killed during a police operation, along with five other police officers, and that it was the worst incident of the kind for well over half a century. Last night they said there was a suspect they were looking for, but they didn't give any further details."

Jenkins guessed that the suspect the police were searching for was almost certainly himself. He knew he had to be extremely cautious in what he told Julie. "Are you sure you want to know more details?" he asked.

Julie nodded. "Yes, I am. Please tell me what you know."

"The Commissioner died instantly from a single gunshot," said Jenkins. "And the man who killed him was then himself killed.........by me."

Julie was surprised. "Really? On the news, there was no mention of anybody else other than the six policemen being killed."

"Yes, I know," said Jenkins. "But in addition to the policemen there were also six dead gunmen. Unfortunately, by the time more police arrived their bodies had been removed, presumably by unknown accomplices."

Julie was puzzled. "But if you were there when Andrew was killed, surely, if any bodies were removed you would have seen who removed them?"

Jenkins was now wishing he hadn't started his explanation. "I was there when Sir Andrew was killed and I shot the man who did it. But then I had to leave the scene very quickly because I was responsible for protecting someone else. I don't know what happened after I left."

Before Julie could follow up with any more questions about the events at the farmhouse, Jenkins quickly moved to the subject of Sir Andrew's unofficial report. "When Sir Andrew came to visit you last Friday, I believe he may have brought a black folder with him. Did he leave it here with you?"

"Yes, I know what you mean," said Julie. "It's in a drawer upstairs. I'll go and get it."

Whilst Julie was out of the room Jenkins examined the card that had been delivered with the flowers. It read, 'Happy Anniversary, darling. Love Andrew xx'. He also took the opportunity to take a good look around the room he was in. It appeared ordinary enough, but one thing about it did strike him as unusual – there were no photographs of any kind to be seen. He couldn't recall ever before going into a home's main reception room and not seeing at least a couple of family photographs on display.

When Julie returned with a folder Jenkins quickly thumbed through it and confirmed it was the one he was referring to. "Did Sir Andrew say anything about this file?" he asked.

Julie shook her head. "Not really, only that it was a confidential document he wanted me to keep here for the time being. Given the situation as it is now, though, you might as well have it. As I said, I know he trusted you."

During their meeting Jenkins formed a very positive view of Julie. Perceiving her to be honest and open, he saw no reason why he should disbelieve or doubt anything she told him. If he was going to find out who divulged the whereabouts of the safe-house he became convinced he would have to look elsewhere.

After insisting that Julie keep the photographs, Jenkins finished his tea and was on the point of leaving, when one last thought occurred to him. "You might like to know the Commissioner received the birthday present you sent him. I was with him when it arrived around lunchtime on Monday. It was obvious he liked the pen very much."

Julie looked puzzled. "I didn't send Andrew a pen. It didn't come from me. I gave him a birthday gift whilst he was here at the weekend. I'd teased him once or twice about the ties he usually wore. I said they suggested he was dressed for a funeral, because they were all so very dark and somber. For his birthday I gave him a really colourful one and then insisted he wore it."

Jenkins had borrowed Brazelle's jeep for his trip to Eastbourne and had parked it on the road directly in front of Julie's cottage. When he came to leave there was just one other car in the quiet road. It was stationary about fifty metres away, but with its engine still running. Jenkins would probably have thought nothing more about it, but as he drove off he glanced into his rear view mirror and saw the previously immobile car begin to slowly move forward. By the time he reached the end of the road it had again come to a stop, this time in the space that he had just vacated, immediately in front of Julie's cottage.

Back at Holford's Cottage, Jenkins gave Brazelle a report of his meeting with Julie and how he'd concluded she was an innocent party who knew nothing about the safe-house. Initially he didn't mention the car he'd seen outside her cottage, or the puzzling issue of the pen, but later, as both matters continued to play on his mind, he decided that he should. Although there could have been an entirely innocent reason to explain the behaviour of the car, Jenkins was far more inclined to believe it was the action of someone who was planning on paying Julie a visit, but didn't want him to know about it. "I have the feeling it was deliberately keeping just far enough away, so I couldn't see the driver or clock the registration," he said. "I can't even be certain what make of vehicle it was, although if I had to hazard a guess I'd say it was a large Merc. And it was definitely black."

Brazelle laughed. "Well that should narrow it down to a few million possibilities. Anyway, although it may be of absolutely no consequence and most other people probably wouldn't have given it a second thought, the car's behaviour clearly registered with you."

As a police officer Jenkins was trained to be observant, but since becoming a fugitive he'd noticed that his observational skills had sharpened up even more. "I hope I'm not becoming paranoid," he said. "Increasingly, I seem to get suspicious over things which, to most other people, would probably appear to be of no real importance, just trivial and insignificant matters."

Brazelle was reassuring. "In the situation we currently find ourselves, a bit of suspicion might be no bad thing. Neither, by the way, is a touch of paranoia! Remember there really are people out to get you. And experience has taught me, as

I'm sure it's taught you, that sometimes the small and seemingly insignificant detail can turn out to be the key to solving the bigger problem. But tell me about the pen. Why do you think that might be important?"

Jenkins frowned. "When we found out about Julie I just assumed that it came from her. Remembering how the Chief reacted when he received it and then read the card that came with it, I reckon that's what he was thinking as well. But today Julie assured me that she hadn't sent it. So who did? Maybe within the great scheme of things it's of no real importance, but it's a loose end. And I don't like loose ends."

Brazelle was of the same mind. "And you're not the only one who doesn't like them. But where's the pen now?"

"The Chief had it in his pocket at the safe-house. It was most probably destroyed in the fire, but if there was anything left of it, it'll be with forensics."

Brazelle switched on the TV to catch the news. He assumed that the killing of six police officers would still be the lead item. But it wasn't. It had been replaced by the news that a fifty two year old woman had been found murdered in her home in Eastbourne earlier that day. A television journalist was giving his report from the street where the victim lived and, although she wasn't named, Jenkins instinctively knew who she was.

The two men watched the rest of the report in silence. When it ended Jenkins was the first to speak. "Why the hell would anyone want to kill Julie? And the way things stand I'm very quickly going to become the number one suspect.

My fingerprints will be all over the place. And it won't take the investigators long to find out I was asking about her at Leonardo's. When they discover that she was in a relationship with the Commissioner, they'll probably think there's some connection to what happened at the safe-house and assume it's an open and shut case."

Brazelle agreed. "I doubt it'll be long before they decide to publicly name you. In fact I can't understand why they haven't done that already. And why haven't they made it public that they've lost Gant? They won't be able to keep the lid on any of this for much longer. And when they do finally get around to publicly naming you, you won't be safe here. For a start there's Gerald Caulfield to consider. So far he hasn't committed any crime. All he's done is treat an injured police officer who, at the time, had legal custody of a prisoner. Once your name's put out as a murder suspect, though, he'll have to report it, or he'll be guilty of withholding evidence. And that is a crime."

"Did you touch the photographs I gave Julie?" asked Jenkins. "Are your fingerprints likely to be on them?"

Brazelle shook his head. "No. I'm quite certain you were the only one who handled them."

"But I was driving your jeep," said Jenkins. "That could be traced back to you."

"Not necessarily," responded Brazelle, "but even if someone did connect you to the jeep, that doesn't guarantee that its registration was recorded or it was caught on CCTV. And even if the jeep is identified, it doesn't directly lead back to me. It's owned by the Harfield

Estate, not by me. The previous occupier of this cottage was one of the Estate's employees and seems to have been the main user of the jeep. He kept it here in one of the outbuildings and when I moved in it was still there, although it was a non-runner. I did a deal with the Estate Manager - if I could get it going, then I could use it, but I'm far from being the only authorised driver. As well as me any employee of the Harfield Estate who has a driving licence is authorised and insured to drive it. I'm not even the registered keeper, despite it normally being parked in the outbuilding where I found it. Theoretically there is a very long list of people who could have been driving the jeep. The Estate Manager is currently on leave, climbing mountains somewhere in the Himalayas and, as far as I'm aware, Rose and Max are the only other people who know that I normally keep the jeep here at Holford. If I parked it round the back of the Harfield Estate office, I doubt that anyone could be certain where it had been, or list all those who might have been driving it during the past six months, let alone the past few days."

"Is that what you intend to do?" asked Jenkins.

Brazelle gave a faint shrug. "I suppose I'll have to. I'll miss it though. It's been very useful these past few months. But I'll still have my Ferrari." Brazelle had won the Ferrari off a Lebanese diamond trader in a high stakes poker game several years earlier. Other than his relationship to Max, it was the only link that remained to his former life."

Jenkins frowned. "I thought you owned the jeep. It now seems I've been driving it without the owner's consent. That's an offence."

If the situation had not been so serious, Brazelle might have burst out laughing. "I can't believe what you just said, Ifor. With what you've got hanging over your head and you're worried about driving a vehicle without the owner's consent. But if it makes you feel any better, I'm sure I can get one of the Harfield sisters to give you their retrospective permission."

Day Five - Friday

Brazelle woke just before seven. His first action was to turn on the radio and listen to the seven o'clock news. Not surprisingly, Julie's murder was still a major item. It was reported that police were linking her death to the killing of six police officers a few days earlier and were looking for the same person in connection with both crimes. It was obviously Jenkins they were referring to, but the bulletin ended without mentioning him by name. Brazelle was relieved, although he knew the situation could change at any moment. Entering the sitting room, he found his guest had already prepared breakfast.

Jenkins placed two large plates of food on the table. "I thought it was time I made a contribution in the comestibles department," he said. "I got up early and shot down to the village shop to get some stuff. I picked up some newspapers at the same time. Julie's murder is the lead story for all of them. None of them has much more to report than we heard on the news last night, except to say that she was strangled."

When the two men finished their breakfast Brazelle commended Jenkins on his culinary skills. "That was excellent. There's definitely evidence of an alternative career possibility if you ever decide to give up police work."

"Well that's as maybe," said a rather downbeat Jenkins. "I only hope it isn't a job in a prison canteen."

Brazelle was considering how he might raise Jenkins' spirits, when Coyte-Sherman arrived with some progress to report. "We found Gant's wife and took her to see him. He now claims to be keeping his word by telling us everything he knows, but we know he's a crafty bastard who's very experienced in the dark arts, so nobody's getting too excited just yet. Where we have been able to verify what he's given us so far, though, it does seem to stack up. For a start, he gave up a safe-house in London that we knew nothing about. Whether or not the Security Service knew about it, I don't know. Cross referencing anything with them will have to wait until we eventually own up to having Gant. He also claimed there was a spy at NATO HQ. Although he didn't have a name, he knew it was a middle ranking Dutch officer who'd been in post for about two years. We passed on the information, but without giving away the identity of the source, of course. It turns out there were already suspicions that one particular unit had a mole. And a live investigation was already underway with well over a hundred potential suspects. Gant's information got that narrowed down to just one man and he's now under arrest and being interrogated in Brussels. Gant also told us how he got involved with the organisation in the first place. It was during his early days in MI5 after he'd acquired a rather unfortunate and expensive gambling habit. He'd got himself into a load of debt and knew it was only a matter of time before it got picked up by his superiors and he'd get fired. When he was approached with an offer of having his gambling debts paid off with some money to spare, he took it. After that, it appears he became hooked on the idea of easy money. But that wasn't his only reward. Every now and again the organisation fed him snippets of information. It was stuff that was of no further use to them, but material that helped make him look good in the eyes of his bosses.

The organisation must have seen him as someone worth investing in for the future. And it seems their investment paid off.........well, until now at least. He says the only things he won't talk about are his own acts of espionage, although we haven't closed the book on those matters just yet."

Brazelle was only marginally impressed. "Well that certainly bolsters Gant's credentials as a turncoat informer, but it seems to me there's nothing there that will identify Austin and tell us who divulged the whereabouts of the safe-house. I know you too well, Danny. You didn't come all the way here just to tell us something that you could have mentioned in a phone call. Why are you really here?"

Coyte-Sherman smiled. "Nothing gets passed you, does it, Chris? So I'll get to the tricky bit. Unfortunately, some of what Gant's told us can only be checked out with the help of the CIA. But knowing how you feel about that particular agency, I thought I should talk to you first, before I make contact. But trust me Chris. I know exactly who I'll be dealing with. He's a personal friend of mine. We worked together for a while in the Middle East when he was with US Military Intelligence. A couple of years ago he left the army and went to work for the CIA as a senior analyst in Langley. And what I need to check with him really is important. If Gant is telling the truth then it's something that could blow the whole thing wide open. He says the organisation is headed jointly by a small group, rather than a single individual. And although it was just the once, he heard the group referred to as 'The Triumvirate'. I know he could be lying and stringing us along, but he's given us some very precise Intel to support his claim. That's why I need to contact the CIA. We'll need their help to confirm it all stacks up and, with a bit of luck, identify not just Gant's handler and Austin, but maybe all three members at the top of the organisation as well."

Brazelle was dubious. "When I spoke to Gant the other day he claimed to have fairly low status in the organisation, so how would he get to know any of this?"

Coyte-Sherman's response was to play an extract of a recorded statement that Gant had given.

"It was July 7th, four years ago, just after I'd been promoted to Deputy Director of MI6. I remember it so well because it was our wedding anniversary and my wife and I were out in town having a celebratory dinner together. Half way through our meal I got a message from my handler, demanding that I meet with him urgently. Apart from Orlando, he was the only other person connected with the organisation I'd ever met face to face, but such meetings were very rare events and always extremely brief. He asked me to meet him in the same place where we always met, on a particular bench in Regent's Park, at exactly nine o'clock. But he turned up several minutes late. When he eventually arrived he was carrying an overnight bag and a briefcase. After apologising for being late, he took an envelope from his briefcase and gave it to me, saying it was from the people at the very top of the organisation. It contained a list of information requirements and details of an offshore bank account. I was told that I was now an even more valuable asset and would in future receive more generous rewards, which would be deposited into the offshore bank account. During our conversation I noticed that his speech was slightly slurred. I was already annoyed at having been dragged away from the anniversary dinner with my wife. And concluding that I'd been kept waiting because he'd been drinking, I became extremely angry. He said he'd come straight from Heathrow in a taxi, having just flown directly back from New York where he'd met with the 'Triumvirate', as he called them, and he apologised for perhaps having drunk a little too much on the plane."

"Gant's handler sounds unbelievably polite", said Jenkins when the playback ended. "Apologising for being late and then for having drunk too much on the plane! Is any of this credible?"

"He's obviously Public School educated," said Brazelle. "Even if they've come to put a bullet in your head, if they turn up late, or drunk, they'll still apologise first. They never forget their manners."

"I went to a Public School!" Coyte-Sherman objected.

Brazelle grinned. "And doesn't it show. But, please go on, Danny. Did Gant give any other details about his handler?"

After muttering some profanity Coyte-Sherman continued. "He said he knew him only by the codename Seattle. And that he's white, about forty years of age and speaks English with an American, New England accent."

"It seems to me you've probably got enough there to identify Seattle," said Brazelle. "Assuming Gant and his handler were both telling the truth of course."

"I think we might be part of the way there already," said Coyte-Sherman. "Only two planes arrived at Heathrow from New York within the relevant time frame on that particular day. Fortunately we were able to get hold of the passenger list for both flights. After eliminating women and children and all the men with dates of birth well outside the possible range, we were initially left with thirty-nine possibilities. We've now managed to whittle it down to just three, all American citizens. If we're going to narrow it down any further we'll need the help of the CIA."

"Why has it got to be the CIA?" Brazelle asked. "Why not use your contacts in US Military Intelligence, or even the FBI?"

Coyte-Sherman shook his head. "No chance. The American Constitution strictly forbids all branches of the US Military getting involved in anything domestic and civilian. And the FBI will only do business through the approved channels. That means MI5 or the police and, for obvious reasons, that's not possible at the moment."

"Yes, of course," said Brazelle with a hint of sarcasm, "I was forgetting how long a shadow the ghost of J. Edgar Hoover still casts over the FBI. He was always a stickler for playing by the rules. The CIA, of course, doesn't have any rules."

Thinking it might be a good idea to move the subject away from the CIA, Coyte-Sherman turned his attention to Jenkins. "We haven't yet come up with any plausible theory as to why your attackers were kitted out with Met gear, but we're pretty sure we know where the dagger came from. The writing on the handle and what you heard the Commissioner's killer say, dink weer, means, 'think again'. It's the Afrikaans motto of a freelance South African mercenary outfit. It rang a distant bell when you told me about it the other day. Then when I started checking it out

I discovered where I'd come across it before. This particular crew came onto MI's radar for the first time about five years ago. At the time we classified them Level Four and they've stayed at that level ever since. If it turns out that it really was them who staged the attack on the safe-house we'll have to upgrade them, probably to Level Two."

"Level Four? Level Two?" queried a puzzled Jenkins. "What exactly does all this mean?"

Brazelle gave the explanation. "They're classifications given to organised and well resourced armed groups that have no permanent allegiance to any particular state. Some are motivated by political or religious beliefs, but many of them are just freelance mercenary outfits who'll work for just about anybody who's willing and able to pay. If they're graded at Level Four, it means they're not currently seen as a direct threat to the UK or its citizens. There are God only knows how many of those around the world at any particular time and their actions are just monitored. At Level Three they risk getting taken out by our military only if they get too close for comfort. But at Level Two we actually go looking for them. And then we take them out. That's what my unit used to do."

"And what about Level One?" asked Jenkins.

Coyte-Sherman chose to answer. "It means they're perceived to be such a serious threat they'll be taken out urgently, often with only limited consideration given to the potential for collateral damage. Air strikes; cruise missiles; drones; almost anything might be used against them."

"But a Level One classification is given very infrequently," interrupted Brazelle.

"Very true," said Coyte-Sherman. "Although they do seem to be getting ever more common......Anyway Chris, about contacting my friend at the CIA, do you approve?"

"I think 'approve' might be going too far," Brazelle replied. "Let's just say that I'll 'tolerate'. But I have another favour to ask. Can you find somewhere for Ifor to stay for a while? It's only a matter of time before he's publicly named as someone the police are looking for in connection with what is now seven deaths. Given the amount of public interest, the pressure to do that must already be enormous. And when it does happen, he won't be safe here."

Although he hadn't been consulted on the matter, Jenkins agreed with Brazelle's assessment of his situation and did not object.

After driving off from Holford's Cottage, Coyte-Sherman explained to Jenkins why Brazelle displayed such antagonism towards the CIA and how it had its roots in something that happened in Iraq several years earlier. "The CIA had members of its own private army all over the place. Some of them thought they were living in the Wild West and created all kinds of problems. But one event, in particular, really did it for Chris. A unit of CIA contractors raided a village a few miles north of Basra, claiming they had intelligence that a couple of people they were looking for were hiding out there. When they didn't immediately find who they were looking for they started getting rough with some of the villagers. Chris's unit had recruited an interpreter from the village several months earlier and when all this happened he was at home there. When it started to turn nasty he tried to intervene. We never found out exactly what happened next, but at some point one of the contractors shot and killed him. When Chris heard what had happened he and his unit went after the contractors and eventually caught up with them."

"And then what happened?" asked Jenkins.

Coyte-Sherman took his eyes off the road for a moment and stared at Jenkins with a look of near disbelief. "It was a fucking war. What do you think happened?"

The rest of the journey passed in silence.

The Harfield Estate Management Office is located on the Prinsted Village High Street in premises that were once home to a bank. Brazelle deliberately arrived at the Office when he knew it would be closed, parked his jeep in a small private car park at the rear of the building and posted the vehicle's keys through the letterbox. Reluctantly, he had accepted he could no longer keep the jeep at Holford. If anyone reported seeing such a vehicle parked outside Julie's cottage on the day of her murder he assumed it would only be a matter of time before it was eventually identified.

And of course the police might not be the only people searching for the jeep. Brazelle was convinced that Julie's killer was in the car that pulled up outside her cottage just after Jenkins drove away. If he was right, then the murderer would have had ample opportunity to note the jeep's registration number and might have their own reasons for wishing to locate its driver.

Brazelle knew he could not erase all evidence of his own connection to the jeep, but before leaving it parked behind the Estate Management Office he made a good attempt at removing any evidence that might connect it to Jenkins. He did not consider what he was doing to be in any way impeding the police investigation into Julie's murder or, for that matter, the events that had taken place at the safe-house. It was his firm belief that Jenkins was an innocent man and his actions were simply an attempt to buy time until the real killers could be identified. He was hoping to stall matters for a while, giving Coyte-Sherman and his team more time to come up with answers.

After abandoning the jeep, Brazelle walked over to Harfield House, the Georgian mansion that stood in its own extensive grounds on the northern edge of the village, surrounded by a high stone wall, referred to locally as Napoleon's Wall. It was home to Rose and her much older half-sister, Frances, daughters of the late Sir Cornelius, the 11th Baronet Harfield; and, Frances's husband, the senior diplomat, Sir Damien Marshall.

Informed by the butler, Jonathan Richards, that Lady Frances was busy in the basement, Brazelle went down unannounced to join her.

With the assistance of the housekeeper, Jonathan's wife Megan, Frances was sorting through a numerous and varied collection of paintings, artefacts and general detritus that had been allowed to accumulate in the basement over decades, if not centuries. Both women had attempted to dress appropriately for the task. Frances was wearing paint splattered overalls that were clearly a few sizes too big for her, with rolled up sleeves and trouser legs. Brazelle was surprised by the sight. It was the first time he had ever seen her dressed in anything other than haute couture.

As Frances became aware of Brazelle's unexpected arrival she immediately guessed what he might be thinking. "They were my father's overalls," she said. "To say he was not a small man would be an understatement. If they'd actually fitted I would have been mortified."

Brazelle smiled. "I'm a great believer in utility taking precedence over appearance, Frankie. One should always try and dress appropriately for any occasion. I'd say you've scored a ten."

Frances returned Brazelle's smile. "I won't ask what the ten is out of. Anyway, it's nice to see you, Chris. And you may have arrived at just the right time. Are you any good at picking locks?"

Brazelle gave a slight shrug. "From time to time I have managed to open the occasional lock without a key, but I certainly wouldn't claim to be an expert locksmith." He was understating his achievements. In the past, he had in fact succeeded in opening a considerable number of locks without the use of a key, although it had usually been with the aid of Semtex, C-4 or some other type of explosive. On this occasion, however, he made the reasonable assumption that Frances had a much gentler technique in mind. "What is it that you want opening?" he asked.

Frances pointed to a large wooden trunk. "It's that. Neither Megan nor I remember ever seeing it before, but I suppose that's not too surprising. My father was a hoarder, as was his father before him. They both used to store all kinds of things down here and discouraged anyone from tampering with them. I've spent so much time away from Harfield House in the twenty years since my father died, it's only now that I've got round to going through it all. Some of this stuff, including the trunk, appears to be very old, so I guess hoarding must be a Harfield family trait going back a lot further than my grandfather. We found it tucked away in a corner with all sorts of things on and around it. It probably hasn't seen the light of day for decades. I'd love to know what's in it, but unfortunately it's locked and we haven't been able to find the key."

Brazelle inspected the lock. "It doesn't look to be particularly sophisticated. I should be able to get it open with the aid of a screwdriver."

Gareth, Mrs. Richards' thirty one year old son, had had the use of a basement storeroom since it was allocated to him by Sir Cornelius Harfield, Frances's and Rose's late father, more than twenty years previously. He used it to store all manner of things including a variety of tools. His mother, who knew this, opened his storeroom door and called out his name, but there was no response. Gareth was nowhere to be seen, much to Mrs. Richards' surprise. "That's odd. I felt sure Gareth was in here. I saw him come in just before you arrived, Reverend. He must have come out and gone back upstairs without me noticing, although I haven't been more than ten feet away from this door in all that time."

Frances also thought it strange. "We must be very absorbed in what we're doing, Megan. I also saw him go in, but never noticed him leave."

After finding what he needed in Gareth's store-room it took Brazelle barely a minute to get the trunk open. But before lifting the lid, he made a show of building up the suspense, which unfortunately only deepened the disappointment when the trunk turned out to be completely empty.

Frances gave out a sigh. "Well, that was a bit of an anti-climax. I was hoping to find something really interesting in there."

There was a Coat of Arms painted on the lid of the trunk and although it was somewhat faded, it was clearly not that of the Harfield family. "Perhaps you have found something interesting, although not inside the trunk," said Brazelle. "This Coat of Arms on the lid, do you know which family that belongs to?"

Frances shook her head. "Not a clue. I'm sure I've never seen it before."

"There's another one over there," said Mrs. Richards, pointing to a second lid that carried the same Coat of Arms. In fact it was identical to the first lid in all other respects as well, except for one obvious difference – there was no sign of the trunk to which it must once have been attached.

Brazelle took a closer look at the unattached lid and a thought occurred to him. "There's an old trunk without a lid in what remains of the basement of the Old House. I remember seeing it when I went down there with Gareth a few weeks ago. I think there's a good chance that this is its missing lid."

"Well there's one way to find out," said Frances. "Shall I ask Jonathan to bring the trunk to the lid, or take the lid to the trunk?"

"Neither, if you don't mind, Frankie," replied Brazelle. "I'd like to check it out myself."

"As you wish," said Frances. "I'll go and find the keys to the old basement for you."

Mrs. Richards looked at her watch. "And it's coming up to Gareth's lunchtime. I'd better go and sort something out for him."

Frances and Mrs. Richards had been extremely busy in the basement over the previous couple of days, establishing structure and order where previously there had been clutter and disorder bordering on chaos. Gathered together in one corner were several old family heirlooms they had uncovered. Brazelle found one of these, the portrait of a young woman, particularly intriguing and was studying it quite intently, when the sound of a door opening broke his concentration and he instinctively turned to look.

Gareth was coming out of his storeroom. Clearly taken by surprise when he saw Brazelle, he stared at him in silence for a moment, before eventually turning away and disappearing up the basement stairs.

Brazelle was puzzled. There had been no sign of Gareth in the storeroom when his mother had gone in there just a few minutes earlier. And Brazelle certainly hadn't noticed him enter since then. Had he simply missed seeing Gareth go in? Or, had Gareth been in there all the time but, for some inexplicable reason, kept himself hidden? Or.........? Intending to return to consider the conundrum later, Brazelle turned his attention back to the portrait of the young woman. He became so engrossed that he didn't immediately notice when someone else entered the basement.

"Beautiful, isn't she?" said a voice from behind.

Brazelle instantly turned. "Yes, she is," he said. "And I have a sudden feeling of déjà vu. I was studying the portrait of a beautiful young woman the last time you got my attention with those same words."

Frances smiled and nodded. "Yes, I remember it well. It was in the library during your first visit to Harfield House. On that occasion it was the portrait of Rose's mother, Justine, that held your interest and I was able to tell you who she was. Unfortunately I can't be any help this time. I haven't a clue who the woman is and I have no recollection of ever seeing her portrait before. We found it carefully wrapped up under several protective layers and hidden away right at the back of everything else down here."

"Hidden?" queried Brazelle. "Do you think your father knew it was down here?"

"Oh, I'm sure he did," Frances replied. "On more than one occasion my mother asked him to clear out this basement and get rid of what she called, 'that rubbish', but his response was always the same. He said he knew exactly what was down here and that none of it could reasonably be described as rubbish. It's true my father was a hoarder, but he was a very well organised one. Anyway, since you seem to have taken an interest in it, perhaps you'll be able to bring your brilliant observational and investigative skills to bear on the matter and come up with some suggestions as to who the woman in the portrait might be. If I was a gambling woman, I'd bet she's a Harfield."

"And if I was a gambling man, I just might take your wager," Brazelle replied. "She may have married into the Harfield family, but I doubt very much that she was born into it. The portrait's dated 1681 and the woman looks to be around twenty years of age, so she must have been born a long time before the establishment of the Harfield dynasty here in Prinsted in 1685."

"Yes, that does seem to confirm that I've just lost my bet," said Frances. "Well spotted. Have your keen observational skills picked up on anything else worth mentioning?"

Brazelle pointed to the bottom right hand corner of the portrait. "That's the signature of Sir Godfrey Kneller who, from 1680 until well into the reign of George the First, held the rather long-winded title of Principal Painter in Ordinary to the English Royal Court. He was a popular and quite prolific portrait painter, although according to many modern art critics, not a particularly good one. The late Brian Sewell, for example, was particularly acerbic and said he used to have to lie down to recover if he ever had to look at more than a couple of Kneller's at a time. Nevertheless, for more than forty years Kneller was the number one portrait artist of choice for those who wanted their 'brush with immortality' and had the money to pay for it."

Frances was impressed. "I already knew you had amazing powers of observation Chris, but now I see you're also something of an expert on seventeenth century portraiture."

"I'm a long way from being an expert," responded Brazelle. "It's pure serendipity. I recently decided to paint a portrait of Rose, although it's intended to be a surprise, so she doesn't know about it yet. Not having had much experience of portrait painting I decided to do some research on the subject and Kneller's name came up. One thing I do know, though, is that portrait painting has never been just about creating a likeness of the subject. Particularly in Kneller's time, a portrait was intended to reflect the subject's personality, their interests and accomplishments and, most of all, their status. In order to achieve that, the artist included all kinds of props and symbols in their painting and this portrait's full of them. I'm surprised your father kept it hidden away down here instead of having it on display somewhere in the House."

Frances was equally surprised. "Yes, it does seem odd, doesn't it? From what you say it would make quite a conversation piece."

"Maybe that was the problem," said Brazelle. "Perhaps your father didn't want anyone conversing about it. Anyway, I think it's a particularly intriguing portrait and I'd really like to understand a bit more about it. Would you mind if I took it away and studied it for a couple of days?"

"Not at all," said Frances. "In fact I'd be very pleased if you did. I'm sure if anyone can find out who the woman is, it's you."

Brazelle smiled. "Well I'll do my best. But I also have another request, and it's the main reason I came here today. I'd like to borrow Rose's car. She's already given me her permission, but I haven't got the keys."

"Yes, of course. It's only parked doing nothing," said Frances. "Is there something wrong with your Ferrari?"

Brazelle shook his head. "No, the Ferrari's absolutely fine, but it does tend to get noticed quite a lot and there are a few things I want to do without attracting too much attention. In any case, I'll be going down to Heathrow to pick up Rose next week. I know she's planning on having most of her stuff shipped over, but she's still going to bring several pieces of luggage with her on the plane. I doubt I'd have enough room in the Ferrari for everything."

"I'll ask Jonathan to bring her car round to the front of the House and put this portrait in it." Frances handed Brazelle a torch and the keys to the old basement. "I won't come with you if you don't mind, Chris. I haven't been down there since I was in my teens, but I can still remember how it gave me the creeps. I'm going to get changed and have some tea in the drawing room. Come and join me when you've finished down there."

The old basement is a subterranean chamber under the southwest corner of Harfield House. It is all that remains of the late seventeenth century mansion built by Sir Richard, the first Baronet Harfield. Everything else was demolished when the new Harfield House was built a century later by Sir Bernard, the fourth Baronet. Access to it is through an external door at the rear of the existing building and down an unlit stone stairway. It is a dark and uninviting place. Following his previous and only other visit Brazelle had been left puzzled as to why Sir Bernard had chosen to retain it. On that occasion, Gareth, the only member of the household who appeared to have any interest in the place, had acted as his guide, but this time Brazelle went down alone.

As Brazelle had suspected, the trunk without a lid that he remembered seeing in the old basement chamber was identical to the one recently discovered. And the spare lid fitted it perfectly. His original purpose for visiting the old basement was now fulfilled but, before leaving, there was one further mystery Brazelle hoped to solve. He consulted a rough sketch he'd made of the layout of the whole of the basement of Harfield House. The outline of the old basement chamber he was standing in was drawn in the southwest corner and he'd pencilled in where he imagined Gareth's storeroom would be in relation to it.

During Brazelle's previous visit to the chamber Gareth had shown him a hidden compartment concealed behind its wood panelling. Tapping the wall, searching for draughts and examining any gaps, however small, Brazelle explored to see if he could find any more. He was convinced that sooner or later he would find something of interest and eventually he did. Through probing in just the right place he found that a part of the panelling opened up to reveal a narrow passageway about six feet high and ten feet long, just wide enough for him to get through. At its far end there was a wooden panel with a small lever attached. Brazelle pressed on the lever, the hinged panel swung away from him, and he stepped forward into Gareth's storeroom.

Brazelle joined Frances in the drawing room where the maid, Layla, was delivering tea and cakes. He intended to report his findings although, for the time being, he was going to leave out any mention of the hidden passageway he'd discovered.

Frances was interested to hear what Brazelle had to say, but there was also another matter she wanted to raise with him. "Do you know what's been happening with Ted Gant?" she asked. "It's been four weeks since the news of his arrest was made public and there was the inevitable news frenzy. Since then, though, we haven't heard anything new, just the same stuff endlessly repeated. Having said that, I'm very glad there hasn't been any mention of his connection with Prinsted, or to any of us. And you don't think there's any link with what's happened to Sir Andrew Carpenter, do you? Things are being kept very tight. Despite his senior position at the Foreign Office, even Damien hasn't been able to find out anything. But I thought that with your....... shall we call them 'unofficial' channels of communication, you might know something more than the rest of us."

Brazelle was cautious in his response. "I think you might be overestimating the strength of my connections. But I do have it on good authority that Sir Andrew went out of his way to ensure there was no reference to Gant's links to Prinsted in anything that was made public. He assumed it was what we all wanted and reckoned he had enough evidence to ensure that Gant went away for life without having to mention his connection to any of us. The lack of recent news on the case is understandable, I suppose, given how embarrassing it's been for the Government. They've probably been keen to let as little as possible get out. There most likely hasn't been any fresh news for the mainstream media to report since Gant was first arrested. Even his current whereabouts will be kept confidential. We'll probably wake up one morning to find he's already had a trial in secret, been found guilty and sentenced to life. Then it'll just wither away. Except on social media, of course, where no doubt all sorts of conspiracy theories will be proposed and circulated. As to a possible link between Gant and the death of Sir Andrew, I certainly wouldn't rule it out, but we'll probably find out sooner or later."

Having attempted to respond to Frances's enquiries as openly as he thought he could, without giving too much away, Brazelle posed a few questions of his own. "When I was down in the old basement I was reminded of something that Mrs. Richards told me some weeks ago. She said that Gareth was eight years old when your father suggested building a tree house for him, just after he discovered that Gareth had found his way into the old basement. It seems very odd to me that an eight year old would want to go into a dark underground chamber. You said yourself, even as a teenager it gave you the creeps. Did Gareth ever give a reason why he went in there? And how did your father find out that he had been?"

Frances understood how unusual some of Gareth's reported behaviour as an eight year old might appear. "You have to understand that Gareth wasn't a typical eight year old, Chris. Whilst most children that age would have been quite horrified by the thought of going alone into a dark underground chamber, it wouldn't necessarily have the same effect on Gareth. Meeting new people and confronting novel social situations are what unnerve him. I remember my father asking if it was me who'd been down there after he'd discovered that some things had been moved around.

I assured him that I most certainly hadn't. A few days later he said he'd found out that it was Gareth, although he didn't tell me what he'd been doing down there. And I didn't ask. But I remember thinking the whole thing rather odd, just as you do now."

"Presumably your father would have asked Gareth how he got into the old basement."

"Yes, I'm sure he did. And Gareth, being Gareth, would have told him. But I don't remember my father passing on that information to anyone else. I've always assumed that Gareth found out where my father kept his keys and was simply curious about what he might find in the old basement. I suppose he thought it would be a bit of an adventure to visit one of the few parts of the House he'd never been in before."

Brazelle was confident that Gareth had not needed keys to enter the old basement, because he had discovered the secret passageway. He was also quite convinced that Sir Cornelius would have known about the passageway before he gave the storeroom to Gareth. And that puzzled him. Was it just by chance that Sir Cornelius had given him that particular storeroom, or was it a deliberate choice? Did Sir Cornelius want Gareth to find the passageway? Perhaps he even expected him to. Or, was it his intention to tell Gareth about it at some time in the future? Brazelle was convinced that Sir Cornelius knew that Gareth was his biological son and thought it possible, likely even, that he intended to pass on a number of family secrets at some point, but why this particular secret? And, perhaps even more puzzling, why was it a secret?

Brazelle was also curious about Gareth's tree house. "Do you know why your father asked Jonathan to build a tree house for Gareth? It's not exactly the first thing that comes to mind if you're thinking about creating some kind of workshop for a young boy, which seems to be what it quickly became."

"When my father was about twelve years old, my grandfather had a tree house made for him, so I've always assumed that was the reason," replied Frances. "Father probably thought the idea would appeal to Gareth, just as it had to him. And I'm sure it did, because in the twenty three years since it was built he's always spent most of his spare time in there."

"Presumably your father's tree house has long since disappeared," said Brazelle.

"Not necessarily," Frances replied. "Father's hoarding habit and his reluctance to let anything go was fairly wide ranging. His tree house was certainly still in existence twenty years ago, when he died, but what state it might be in today I couldn't say. Very delapidated I would imagine."

Brazelle was puzzled. "That's odd. I've strolled around the grounds here with Rose a few times, but I've never seen any sign of anything resembling a tree house, apart from Gareth's, of course."

Frances smiled. "Well there's a very good reason for that. Father's tree house isn't in the House grounds. It was constructed in the enclosed wooded area that belongs to the Harfield Estate on the other side of Napoleon's Wall, to the west. There's a door through the wall that gives access to it. And it's probably more accurately described as a house in the trees, rather than a tree house. Although it's sited amongst trees and my father gave it the name 'The Tree House' when it was first built, it actually stands on the ground, not up in any tree. I can tell you're interested, so I'll ask Jonathan to bring the key for the door in Napoleon's Wall, and you can go and see whatever remains of it for yourself. Before you do, though, there's something else you might be interested in taking a look at first."

Frances led the way into the library where she extracted a large aerial photograph from the map drawer and laid it out on the table. "This shows how the Harfield House grounds and the surrounding area looked in my grandfather's day. My father's tree house was constructed just about here." She pointed to a small building that was sited in a clearing in the trees.

"When was this photograph taken?" Brazelle asked.

"Sometime during the Second World War, I believe," Frances replied. "Several members of an RAF aerial reconnaissance squadron were billeted in the House during the war and just before they left, one of them took this photograph and gave it to my grandfather as a parting gift."

Brazelle was intrigued. "So it must have been taken before your father's tree house was built. Yet there's very clearly a building of some kind where you just pointed. Do you know what stood there before his tree house was built?"

Frances shook her head. "Not for certain. No. But it was probably a wood-shed. Years ago wood was the main fuel used in the House and most of it came from that wooded area. I suppose it had to be stored somewhere."

Brazelle thought Frances' suggestion was plausible, but there was a second feature showing up on the aerial photograph that also aroused his curiosity. Starting from a point close to the south-west corner of the House, and running in a straight line all the way up to Napoleon's Wall, there was a strip of grass that was very noticeably a different shade of green to that on either side of it. It was impossible to tell if this feature continued in a straight line beyond Napoleon's Wall, because of the many shrubs and trees that covered the ground on the other side, but if it did then it would lead directly to Frances' hypothetical wood-shed, the exact spot that was later to become the site of Sir Cornelius's tree house. Brazelle had observed similar features on aerial reconnaissance photographs during his years in the military and knew what they invariably signalled. This made him even more curious about Sir Cornelius's house in the trees.

A few minutes later Jonathan arrived carrying an ancient looking key ring with two large and equally ancient looking keys hanging on it. "The biggest of the keys is the one you'll need to open the door in Napoleon's Wall," he said, handing it to Brazelle.

"And what does the other one open?" asked Brazelle.

Jonathan reacted with a shrug. "I haven't got the foggiest. It doesn't fit any door in this house. But Sir Cornelius insisted it had to stay on the ring with the other one. So there it remains until somebody tells me otherwise."

Jonathan was dressed casually in sweater and jeans, not in his usual butler's garb. During their brief exchange Brazelle perceived something he thought he'd noticed on more than one occasion before: Jonathan's level of formality always matched that of the clothes he was wearing.

Sir Cornelius's house in the trees turned out to be in much better shape than Frances had suggested it might be. Some of the wall timbers looked like they had recently been replaced and there was a strong smell of wood preservative. Clearly someone had been maintaining it.

The windows were blacked out and closed and the door was bolted and padlocked, but Brazelle was far too curious and impatient to be thwarted by any of this. After opening the largest of the windows with the aid of his penknife he climbed in. The interior was just as well maintained as the exterior and, apart from a half empty tin of wood preservative and several lengths of roughly sawn timber, completely empty.

Two questions began to gnaw at Brazelle. Who was going to the trouble of maintaining this old relic and, even more mystifying, why were they? These were questions he would return to later, but, for the moment, he had a more pressing puzzle to solve.

A thin sheet of vinyl was laid over the floor. Brazelle rolled it back to examine the wooden boards beneath. Within barely a minute he found what he was looking for. There had been an effort to disguise a circular pull-handle as a knot in one of the wooden floorboards. It wasn't the most skilful of attempts, but it still resulted in the handle being so well camouflaged that any casual observer would almost certainly have missed it. Brazelle, of course, was no casual observer.

Beneath the trap door to which the pull-handle was connected was a shaft that went down almost ten feet, with a ladder running down one side. Brazelle climbed down using his phone to light the way. At the bottom was a long, straight, passageway leading off in the direction of the House. Brazelle was too tall to walk along upright, but a little stooping was all that was required. Every so often he paused to inspect the wooden uprights and beams that supported the roof. Most appeared to be many decades old, but some looked like they must have been installed far more recently. Sir Cornelius's house in the trees was clearly not the only construction that was being maintained.

Brazelle travelled along the underground passageway for what he reckoned to be around two hundred yards before it came to an end with what looked very much like a wooden door. He located the keyhole and tried the key for which Jonathan claimed never to have found a lock. It fitted perfectly. The door opened and Brazelle stepped forward into what for him had recently become a very familiar space - the old basement chamber.

Day Six - Saturday

Brazelle woke a few minutes before seven and, just as it had been the day before, his first action was to immediately switch on his bedside radio. He was again relieved when the seven o'clock news bulletin ended without naming Chief Inspector Jenkins.

Despite feeling he could probably have done with another hour's sleep, he forced himself out of bed and began to prepare for what he anticipated would be a very busy day. He was feeling rather sluggish, having burned the midnight oil researching the meaning and significance of the many props and symbols that appeared in the portrait of the young woman. Not only had he consulted his humble, yet authoritative, collection of books dedicated to the history and development of art, but he had made occasional references to appropriately validated and approved internet sites. It had been a night of learning and also one of surprises. By the time he eventually went to bed, he was convinced he had done everything possible to further his research on the woman's portrait and, even better, he believed he had determined who she was.

A few mugs of coffee later, he drove over to Harfield House to return the woman's portrait and explain his findings to Frances, although only with regard to the portrait. He intended to say nothing about any secret passageways, at least for the time being.

Brazelle propped up the portrait of the woman against the drawing room wall. "My research has led me to conclude that this portrait has a fascinating tale to tell," he said. "For a start, it's quite clear that the woman had royal connections."

Frances reacted with surprise. "Whatever makes you think that?"

"A very conspicuous clue," Brazelle replied. "The background in the picture is a wood panelled wall with two paintings on it, paintings within a painting. The one on the left is a simple picture of a vase containing white lilies, but the one on the right is far more complex. It's the portrait of a man with a crown on his head and the seat he's sitting on is a pretty good representation of St Edward's Chair. That's the chair that just about every English monarch since Edward the Second has sat on during their coronation. In 1681, the date of this portrait, Charles the Second was on the throne, so the inference has to be that there was some connection between him and the woman in the portrait. What's more, the miniaturized portrait of Charles the Second that appears in this portrait is a replica of a full size version that Kneller himself had painted a few years earlier."

Frances made a suggestion. "Knowing what we do about Charles the Second, isn't the most likely explanation that the woman in the portrait is one of his many mistresses? Or even possibly his wife?"

Brazelle shook his head. "I think we can discount both those possibilities. The woman is dressed in light blue, her hair is long and loose, and white lilies appear in several places in the painting. All these features were frequently employed as symbols indicating purity, innocence and, most of all, virginity; not things normally associated with King Charles' mistresses. The same features point to it not being Charles' wife either. In any case, there are a number of portraits of Catherine of Braganza with none of them looking anything like the young woman in the portrait and, by 1681, when the portrait was painted, she was much too old."

"Most of the other symbols in the portrait are fairly straightforward and non-controversial, but there are some that I initially found quite puzzling. For a start, there are several indicators that point to the woman being Catholic. She's holding a rosary and laid over the table beside her is a cloth with a Latin script embroidered into it: 'Avarus non implebitur'. That roughly translates as 'A covetous man shall not be satisfied'. It was the motto of Pope Innocent the Eleventh who was Pontiff at the time the portrait was painted. Both the rosary and the script are clear symbols of Catholicism, and their appearance in this portrait struck me as very odd."

"Today it's fairly well established that Charles was a closet Catholic and we know that he formally converted on his deathbed. During his lifetime, though, almost certainly for purely political reasons, he went out of his way to ensure he was never publicly connected to Catholicism. This portrait was created just a year or so after the infamous Popish Plot, during which a lot of innocent Catholics were executed for their alleged involvement. Even Charles' wife, Catherine of Braganza, herself a Catholic, was unfairly implicated and only narrowly escaped being tried for High Treason. At such a time in particular, it would have been extremely bad politics, unthinkable in fact, to have representations of the

King and symbols of Catholicism on display in the same portrait. Kneller, as principal portrait painter to the Royal Court would have known that. In fact, you can be sure he wouldn't have created any portrait with references to the King in it, with or without symbols of Catholicism, unless it was with the King's very clearly expressed permission. Kneller would never have risked displeasing the King. He had far too much to lose. So I think it's reasonable to suppose that the portrait was painted with the consent of the King, although it was probably never meant to be put on public display. It's also logical to conclude that the woman's Catholicism was of great importance to her and, for whatever reason, the King indulged her in her wish to display that in the portrait."

"I'm not aware of any Catholicism amongst our Harfield ancestors," said Frances. "Indeed, our family's founder, Sir Richard, the First Baronet Harfield, was himself an ardent Anglican. Perhaps not surprising given he was raised by an Anglican priest. And as for a possible connection with King Charles the Second, the only association of which I'm aware, is that Sir Richard was an officer in his bodyguard."

"But I haven't finished yet," said Brazelle. "There are two more clues in the portrait that might help to identify the woman. Firstly, her right hand is resting on a book on the table by her side. This suggests, of course, that she is literate. But since the title of the book is, 'La Princess de Clèves', it suggests that she is literate in French. This particular book was published anonymously in 1678, although it's generally assumed to have been written by Marie-Madeleine, Comtesse La Fayette. It's a historical novel that tells the story of a young woman who is married to a wealthy and much older man, but secretly loves a much younger one. Although I've convinced myself that the language of the book is meaningful, I've found it much harder to decide whether or not its subject matter is significant, if only for the fact that the woman is presented as being an unmarried virgin. And secondly, and perhaps most mysteriously of all, the Coat of Arms that appears on each of the two trunk lids you have in your basement also appears on a small shield that's propped up against a table on the far right in the painting."

Frances smiled. "You suspect you know who she is, don't you?"

Brazelle nodded. "I think there's a good chance that it's a portrait of Sir Richard's much younger French wife, Adeline, painted before they were married. Although I still haven't got any clear idea of who she was originally."

"That certainly makes a lot of sense," said Frances, "but what on earth was her connection to King Charles? You don't think she was yet another of his many illegitimate children, do you?"

"I did initially consider that possibility," Brazelle replied. "But there are several reasons why I've now discounted it. The symbols of Catholicism in particular are a real problem. King Charles publicly accepted fathering fourteen illegitimate children, and although there may have been more, this at least shows that formally recognising illegitimate children, of itself, wasn't a particular problem for him. Whether or not the woman in the portrait is Adeline, if she was one of his illegitimate children, why didn't he publicly acknowledge her? After all, he allowed Sir Godfrey Kneller to paint her portrait and include symbols that clearly indicate she had a connection to him, as well as signify and celebrate her Catholicism. This all demonstrates an immense privilege, which was not granted to any of his acknowledged illegitimate children. Charles insisted they were all baptised into the Anglican faith and brought up accordingly. In fact, on the one known occasion that he discovered one of them, a son born to his mistress Barbara Palmer, had been christened a Catholic, he insisted that the child underwent a second, Anglican, baptism."

"That does all sound convincing," said Frances. "But if she isn't one of Charles' illegitimate children, just what is her relationship to him?"

Brazelle was still hopeful of finding an answer. "Well, we do have one or two leads to follow up and one of those is the Coat of Arms that appears on the shield in the portrait and on the trunk lids. You don't happen to know anyone who's into that sort of thing, do you?"

"Off the top of my head, I can't think of anyone," Frances replied. "But Damien's back later today and he might have some suggestions. You'd think that someone in the Diplomatic Service would know a thing or two about heraldry, even French heraldry, or at least know someone who does." Frances' facial expression suddenly changed and she stepped forward to take a closer look at the woman's portrait. "Something has just struck me, Chris. I don't know why I didn't realise it before. I've seen that embroidered cloth and the jewellery the woman is wearing somewhere else in this house. Come with me. I'll show you"

Brazelle followed Frances into the library where his eyes were immediately drawn to the painting that hung over the fireplace, just as they had been on his first entry to that room several weeks earlier. It was a portrait that Sir Cornelius had painted of his second wife, Justine, Rose's mother. And Brazelle very quickly realised what it was that Frances wanted him to see. Justine was wearing the same jewellery as the woman in the portrait: a ring with a large ruby stone, together with a matching pair of earrings and necklace.

"Well that pretty much confirms that your father had seen the jewellery before," said Brazelle. "And I seriously doubt that it was a purely random choice he made to include it in Justine's portrait. Very curious."

"Isn't it just," agreed Frances. "And it gets even more curious. Neither Justine nor I had ever seen the jewellery before. I can still remember how surprised we were when my father unveiled the portrait and we both got to see it for the first time. I asked him where the idea of the jewellery came from. He just pointed at his head and said, "from in here." At the time I assumed he meant it came from his imagination, but now I see that wasn't the case. It came from his memory. But the jewellery Justine is wearing in her portrait isn't all that I wanted to show you. Take a look at the portrait of Sir Bernard, the fourth Baronet Harfield."

Sir Bernard had been painted seated between a large desk and a small table covered by the same embroidered cloth that appeared in the woman's portrait.

"Do you think the appearance of the Pope's motto in the portrait of Sir Bernard indicates that he was also a Catholic?" Frances asked.

"Almost certainly not," replied Brazelle. "There's a Book of Common Prayer sitting on top of it, a clear sign of Anglicanism. I imagine it was placed there deliberately, to counter any thought in the mind of an observer that Sir Bernard might be anything other than a devout Anglican. Perhaps the cloth's appearance in the portrait is due more to an emotional attachment to it rather than a spiritual one. And there's something else in the portrait that looks familiar. I recognise that desk he's sitting alongside as the one in your father's study. It's very distinctive, with something of an oriental look about it."

Frances explained that Sir Bernard had the desk made around the same time he had the original Harfield House demolished and replaced by the Georgian mansion. And how, according to family tradition, both were constructed to Sir Bernard's own design, although there was no evidence that he had received any technical or architectural training.

In his portrait, Sir Bernard was holding a quill pen in his right hand in a way that suggested he was just about to start writing in a book that he was opening with his left. The book had the word 'Journal' written in gold lettering on its front cover.

"It seems Sir Bernard wanted it to be known that he was a keen chronicler," said Brazelle. "Do you know if any of his journals still exist?"

Frances was unsure. "Maybe, but I've never seen one. And I'm fairly certain you won't find one on these library shelves. Many years ago, my mother had an inventory carried out of all the books in here and I don't recall any handwritten diaries or journals appearing on the list. I think the most likely place we'll find them, assuming any still exist, is in my father's studio."

It had been several weeks since Brazelle discovered the true identity of Sir Richard, the First Baronet Harfield, but the identity of his wife Lady Adeline, about whom the Harfield sisters seemed to know very little, remained a mystery. After coming across what he believed to be Adeline's portrait Brazelle's curiosity into her origins had been reignited.

In modern times it is not particularly unusual for the lives of a great-grandmother and her great-grandchildren to overlap, but in the eighteenth century it was highly unusual. In the case of Lady Adeline and her great-grandson, Bernard, who was to become the Fourth Baronet Harfield, their lives had overlapped by an astonishing twenty two years. Brazelle's discovery that Sir Bernard claimed to be a keen diarist led him to consider the possibility that perhaps Lady Adeline had spoken about her early life with her great-grandson and he had kept a written record of such conversations. Maybe he had even made journal entries that would help solve some of the many other Harfield family mysteries. The immediate challenge, though, was to find those journals, assuming they still existed.

Brazelle followed Frances to the top floor of the House and into Sir Cornelius's studio. He cast his eyes around the vast space with its work benches, electronic equipment, artist's paraphernalia and numerous bookshelves.

"It's a daunting task, don't you think?" said Frances. "It'll be like looking for the proverbial needle in a hay-stack."

"What about the House Rules, forbidding the movement of any of your father's stuff?" asked Brazelle.

"Well, they're not so much House Rules as Rose's Rules," replied Frances. "And quite frankly I think it's about time they were changed. I was happy to humour Rose when she was five years old and her mother and our father had just died, but I think it's gone on long enough. I've been meaning to talk to her about it ever since we moved back here after our long absence in the States, but with everything else that's been going on I just haven't got round to it. After sorting through the things in the basement, this studio was the next room on my list for tackling. What we've just discovered is a spur for me to get on with it. As soon as Rose returns from the States I intend to raise the subject with her."

Frances looked at her watch. "Oh dear, I'd quite lost track of the time. I have a lunch date in Northope with a couple of friends and I'm supposed to be meeting them in about fifteen minutes. I'm sorry to have to dash off, Chris, but I'd better get going. Stay here as long as you like and search wherever you want to. I'll tell Megan and Jonathan you're up here and that I've given you permission to move things as you please."

Seconds later Brazelle was alone, wondering where to begin his search, before eventually settling on Sir Cornelius's desk, once owned and allegedly designed by Sir Bernard himself.

The desk displayed a fusion of two characteristic styles: Chippendale and Chinese Qing dynasty. In the mid-to-late eighteenth century it would not have been particularly unusual to find such an item of furniture in the home of a wealthy English gentleman.

Although no expert on antique furniture, Brazelle was aware of the effect that an oriental influence might have on the less obvious aspects of the desk's construction. For one thing, he knew that it was quite common for Chinese furniture makers to include hidden compartments in their creations, especially cabinets and desks. Keeping that in mind, he began by searching through the desk's drawers. None contained anything of interest, but Brazelle discovered that one of the drawers was a good deal shorter than the other five, which were all of identical length.

During his time in the military, Brazelle had often gone in search of things that people didn't want him to find. And these numerous episodes had led him to construct a useful rule-of-thumb: always start with the odd one out. So he did. The short drawer could not be pulled straight out. However, after probing around with his fingers, Brazelle located a release-catch that enabled him to eventually remove it. In the previously hidden space behind he found three books, each labelled 'Journal' in gold lettering, together with a single envelope addressed to Sir Cornelius.

A quick look through the journals confirmed they contained an autobiographical record of events in the life of Sir Bernard, the Fourth Baronet, with each volume covering a period of several years. The earliest of the three volumes also included a dedication, establishing that it had been given to Sir Bernard on the Seventeenth of July, Seventeen Hundred and Fifty Six, as a twenty-first birthday gift from his ninety-seven year old great-grandmother, Adeline. Sir Bernard's career as a diarist appeared to have begun when he received Lady Adeline's gift and, judging by the date of the last entry in the third volume, ended shortly before his death.

Most of the entries in the journals were relatively brief and there were frequent and sometimes quite lengthy gaps between them. Unlike Sir Cornelius, his five times great grandson, it appeared that Sir Bernard was not in the habit of keeping a record of just about everything that happened in his life or every thought that he ever had, regardless of how unimportant or mundane it might be. Brazelle was glad of this. Reading the journals would prove challenging enough. He certainly didn't want to have to plough through pages of trivia.

The envelope addressed to Sir Cornelius bore a post office date stamp confirming it had been posted twenty three years earlier, three years before his death. For Brazelle this was clear evidence that Sir Cornelius knew about the journals but wished to keep their existence secret. And the same appeared to be true of the contents of the envelope.

Frances had given Brazelle permission to go searching for Sir Bernard's journals and, by reasonable inference, consented to him reading them. But the envelope addressed to her father was a different matter. She had made no mention of that.

Brazelle pondered his dilemma, but his curiosity very quickly got the better of him. He opened the envelope and read the letter it contained. By the time he'd finished, however, he almost wished he hadn't. He was still thinking through the potential implications of what he'd just read when his mobile phone rang. It was a number he instantly recognised.

"I thought you'd want to know we've made good progress," said Coyte-Sherman. "With the help of my CIA contact, we've managed to identify Seattle. His name is Vincent Cotham. He's a forty-five year old middle ranking diplomat based at the US Embassy in Nine Elms, here in London. I didn't tell my contact why we were interested in the chap. But he's no fool. He'll know it's not just to satisfy some idle curiosity of mine."

"That really is good news," said Brazelle. "Have you got him under surveillance yet?"

"We're doing our best electronically, picking up bits and pieces of intelligence where we can," replied Coyte-Sherman. "But it would take a dedicated team of at least half a dozen to keep him under twenty-four hour surveillance. And I don't have that level of manpower available. We're pretty stretched as it is. Remember, this is an unofficial operation, Chris. And you can forget about using bugs. Cotham will be scanned whenever he enters the US Embassy, which he does at least once on most days. And he lives in a particularly secure apartment block over-looking Regent's Park, so I doubt we'd get a bug in there either. If we're going to have any chance of tracking his movements and identifying his contacts we'll need to get hold of his phone, without him knowing about it, obviously. Jenkins reckons he knows someone who can get the job done. We're meeting him tomorrow. I'll let you know how we get on."

Despite having to work within tight time constraints and with limited resources, Coyte-Sherman's small team had done a fairly thorough job in their investigation into Vincent Cotham's digital existence. Although a good deal of what they discovered was of no obvious immediate value, some of it, for example information obtained through analysing the record of use of his Oyster Card, proved to be extremely useful. It indicated that on a typical working day Cotham would get on the Tube at Warren Street, just after eight o'clock in the morning, and take the eight minute journey on the Victoria Line to Vauxhall, the nearest tube station to the US Embassy at Nine Elms. It was information which would soon be put to good use.

Fascinating though it may have been, Brazelle was not particularly interested in the generality of Sir Bernard's life story as chronicled in his journals. As he flicked through the pages of the earliest volume, he was hoping to find evidence of something rather specific. Fortunately, quite early on in his quest, he found it. Sir Bernard had made a record of what he claimed was a memoir dictated to him by his great-grandmother, Lady Adeline. It was precisely what Brazelle was hoping to find. Not only had Adeline given details of her origin, but she had also provided a wealth of information that cleared up a number of other Harfield family mysteries. It even appeared to explain the existence of the two passageways that Brazelle had discovered.

It was indeed a vast treasure trove of material.

Or was it?

Brazelle was left with a question. And it was a big one. Was it true? At the heart of what he had read there was a claim, so astonishing and disturbingly problematic, that he considered it to be barely credible.

And there was also the letter he'd found hidden with the journals, with all of its potentially troubling implications. As far as Brazelle knew, only he and the letter's author were aware of its contents, or even of its existence. Did he need to say anything about it to the Harfield sisters? The application of openness and transparency is all well and good, but not at any price. As far as Brazelle was concerned some secrets are best kept secret, especially if revealing them would likely do more harm than good. In the case of the letter, he decided he should ponder the situation a little longer and perhaps even seek advice on the matter, before eventually coming to a conclusion on how to proceed.

And what should he do with the journals? The whole thing was a dilemma, but not one Brazelle could wrestle with indefinitely. There was now very little of Saturday remaining and he had to prioritise how he used what was left of it. Tomorrow was Sunday and he still had a sermon to prepare.

London, Tuesday 12th June 1660. Two weeks after King Charles II's triumphal return to the capital following the ending of Cromwell's Protectorate and the Restoration of the Monarchy

Adam hadn't eaten for two days. Even then it had only been some scraps thrown out by one of the great houses in Whitehall, shared with the feral cats and dogs, not to mention the rats, of the capital. He knew he must eat soon if he was to have any chance of maintaining his health and vigour in this filthy and disease ridden city. But without money, something he did not possess, this was proving to be a mighty challenge. Opening up the pouch that Captain Hadlington had gifted him some nine years earlier he stared at the golden phalera it contained. Knowing its sale would see him well fed, clothed and housed, for a very long time to come, he was sorely tempted. But his adoptive father, the Reverend Shuttleworth, had instilled in him a strong sense of honour and the importance of keeping promises that were freely given. Remembering the pledge he had made to the dying Hadlington, to treasure his most valuable gift, he closed up the pouch and put it back in his pocket.

It was just past mid-day and the summer sun was high in a cloudless sky. Having bartered away his wide brimmed hat in exchange for a loaf of bread several days earlier, Adam had sought protection from the burning sun by seating himself in the shade to the side of one of the city's many narrow streets. The end of this particular street connected with a major thoroughfare and as Adam glanced down to the crossroads he noticed that a large crowd was beginning to form. Inquisitive, he went to join them and on enquiring as to the reason for the gathering was told that the King was expected to pass by soon on his return to Whitehall Palace.

Having lately chosen to keep his interaction with others to a minimum, Adam was not well informed on current royal affairs, or, indeed, on any other matter. But he was aware the monarchy had been restored and that King Charles had recently returned to London from abroad. With nothing better to do, he decided he might as well remain amongst the crowd and also catch a glimpse of the newly returned King. As he looked around for a good place to stand, out of the corner of his eye, he caught a fleeting glimpse of a pistol being passed from the hand of one man to the hand of another. The action was not done openly and took only a split second. Most people would probably have missed it, but Adam was a fugitive and for reasons of self preservation had lately sharpened up his powers of observation. As he continued watching the two men a third came to join them. Adam thought it was very odd, despite the intense summer heat each of the three men was wearing a thick black cloak with his arms concealed inside. He would have persisted with his monitoring of the group but when a loud cheer suddenly went up from the crowd, he was briefly distracted and turned away. A coach pulled by four horses and accompanied by four mounted outriders had turned the corner at the far end of the road and was coming in his direction. Clearly the anticipated arrival of the King, thought Adam, before he turned back to continue with his surveillance, only to find that the three cloaked men had moved. Having pushed their way to the front of the crowd they were standing a few feet apart, some twenty paces to his left.

The coach drew closer, encouraging the crowd to cheer even louder and became ever more animated, but the three men remained motionless and silent. Adam had a deep sense of foreboding and, convinced he knew what was planned, moved to better position himself to prevent it. As the coach reached the point of closest approach the three men suddenly rushed forward, each pulling his arms from under his cloak to reveal two pistols. Shots were fired. The coach was halted as its driver slumped forward. And two of the outriders fell to the ground. A collective shriek of horror went up from the crowd and there was much panic as people scattered in all directions. Adam, though, remained calm. Opening his jacket he revealed that he too was armed. With his pair of pistols drawn he instantly shot dead two of the assailants. The third attacker managed to pull open the coach door, but before he could take aim at the King and pull the trigger of his pistol, Adam grabbed him from behind and thrust a dagger through the man's heart.

The two remaining outriders quickly dismounted. With weapons drawn, they rushed to where Adam was extracting his dagger from the corpse of its victim. Neither man spoke a word to Adam, but looked into the coach to enquire after the King.

"I am unhurt," said the King, "thanks to that young man. Bring him to me."

The men did as instructed and stood alongside Adam by the open coach door.

"I owe you a great debt of gratitude, Master......" The King deliberately paused, waiting for Adam to provide his name.

Adam hesitated. As a fugitive, he was reluctant to reveal his true identity, but glancing over the King's shoulder and through the far window of the coach, he saw a large shop sign, Harfield's Bakery. Almost without thinking he heard himself say, "Harfield, Your Majesty."

The King smiled to himself, having noted Adam's initial hesitation and also the name, Harfield, reflected in the coach window in front of him. "And what is your occupation, Master....... Harfield?" he asked.

Adam again hesitated slightly before eventually giving a reply. "I am currently at leisure, Your Majesty."

The two men standing alongside Adam burst into laughter, but the King cast them both a disapproving look and they at once fell silent.

The King gestured with his hand at the rags that Adam was wearing. "I have been away from England far too long and find myself entirely unfamiliar with the fashion currently being worn by gentlemen at leisure. But tell me, Master Harfield, would you be prepared to give up your life of leisure and your current dress, for a position in my Guard and the wearing of its uniform?"

The stench from his filthy clothes and the rumbling of his empty belly, of which everyone present was only too well aware, prompted Adam to give the only sensible response to the King's proposal. "It would be both a privilege and an honour, Your Majesty."

"Excellent. Then the decision is made," said the King, before turning to the older of his two remaining guards. "Take Master Harfield to the barracks, Colonel. Provide him with food and an opportunity to bathe. Then allocate him a billet and issue him with some clothes, more appropriate for a soldier in my Guard than the gentleman's attire in which he is currently dressed."

The Colonel acknowledged the King's instructions and closed the carriage door.

The entrance to the King's palace and its barracks was little more than two hundred yards further along the road from where the attack had taken place. As soon as the sound of pistol fire and the screaming of the crowd had been heard, scores of soldiers had rushed out, on horseback and on foot, towards the King's coach. By the time the conversation between Adam and the King had concluded, the coach was already surrounded by guards and the dead coach driver had been replaced. The Colonel gave the command and the carriage set off to complete its journey to the palace, but this time accompanied by far more than just the four guards who had travelled alongside it previously. Adam stood by the side of the Colonel and watched until the coach and its entourage eventually disappeared into the palace precincts.

"The King is not the only one who owes you a debt of gratitude, Master Harfield," said the Colonel. "Even if I had survived alive from today's event, if the King had been killed, my life would have been as good as ended. As commander of His Majesty's bodyguard I would have been disgraced. My career would be over and, no doubt, I too would have become a gentleman of leisure." To emphasise his point the Colonel pointed to the filthy rags that Adam was wearing before offering him his hand. "I am Colonel John Aston. What is your christian name Master Harfield?"

Adam had just re-holstered the two pistols and sheathed the dagger that he had inherited from his adoptive father, Richard Shuttleworth, and had him in mind when the Colonel made his enquiry. "Richard," he said, after a momentary pause. "My name is Richard Harfield."

Friday 15th December 1660

Six months after he had saved the King's life and been recruited into his bodyguard, Adam, now calling himself Richard Harfield, had completed his military training. Having excelled in all elements, he had come to be acknowledged as the best marksman in the Regiment and one of its finest swordsmen. He was also regarded as rather reclusive and, whilst not exactly antisocial, one of the Regiment's least affable members. His comrades were all aware of the events that had brought him to be one of their number and why, therefore, he appeared to be something of a favourite of the Colonel as well as highly thought of by the King himself.

Richard's platoon had been given a weekend's leave, their first release from duty for several weeks. Not surprisingly, Richard's comrades had all left the barracks, intending to make the most of it. During the time of Cromwell's Protectorate, so recently ended, all manner of puritanical restrictions had been imposed on the people. With the return of the monarchy, however, practically all constraints had been removed and the fleshpots and taverns of the city were once again thriving, providing Richard's comrades with ample opportunity for merry, and even licentious, release.

Colonel Aston entered the dormitory where Richard and the rest of his platoon were billeted. Being aware of Richard's somewhat reserved nature, the Colonel was not too surprised to find that he was the only member of the platoon still present.

"Not out in the city making merry with your comrades I see, Master Harfield," observed the Colonel. "How do you intend spending your weekend leave? Do you have family to visit?"

"No sir, I have no living family," Richard replied, before placing his hand on a pile of three books that lay on the table in front of him. "I intend to read these. I was permitted to borrow them from the King's library."

The Colonel picked up each of the books in turn and saw that one of them was written in French. "You can read French?" he asked.

Richard nodded. "I was first taught by my father. As I believe I told you, sir, in his younger days he was a soldier in the army of King James. Whilst in the King's service he spent two lengthy periods in France and found it convenient to learn the language. I was also helped in my learning by a French Huguenot family that came to live in our village. The head of the family was a medical man who became my father's closest friend. He had a grandson of similar age to me and we also became good friends. Unfortunately, I have had few opportunities to converse in the language since I left the village after the death of my father, so I have attempted to retain my level of fluency through reading and writing."

"Despite your outstanding soldiering abilities, you are indeed a most unlikely recruit to the humble ranks of the King's Guard, Richard. Very few of your comrades possess any more learning than that which I, myself, have taught them. And much of that is merely how to kill, whilst avoiding being killed themselves. Hardly any one of them has even the most elementary facility with the written word. Yet you are sufficiently accomplished to read and write in two languages, exceeding even the ability of most of my fellow officers. We shall have to see how you develop over the coming months. If you progress well, as I believe that you will, I shall seek His Majesty's approval for giving you a commission."

"Would becoming an officer mean I could move out of this dormitory and have a billet of my own, sir?" Richard asked.

The Colonel smiled, remembering that Richard was someone who tended to prefer his own company. "Most certainly," he replied, "together with a generous uplift in your pay, to boot. And, provided you do not become one for fripperies, you should have enough to maintain a wife and family, as I do. But first you must show your potential for leadership. And perhaps the opportunity to do just that has already arrived. I shall inform the officers of the Regiment that I have promoted you to the rank of corporal with immediate effect and placed you in command of your platoon. Your first challenge will be to ensure that all the men return on time from their period of leave, in a fit state to immediately resume their duties. Anyone who does not should be appropriately dealt with. I have come to inform you now because, on command from His Majesty, I am to leave for France in the morning at first light. I will be gone for several days, although I hope to be home by Christmas. Upon my return I expect to receive only good reports of your conduct during my absence. Is my instruction clear enough, Corporal Harfield?"

Richard stood to attention and saluted. "Totally sir, I will not let you down."

The Colonel returned Richard's salute. "Good. Then I shall leave you to get on with your reading. Enjoy what is left of your period of leave. The next may not come for some time."

Tuesday 15th June 1661

Six months to the day, after Richard had been promoted to the rank of corporal, providing him with an opportunity to demonstrate his leadership skills, the Colonel was as good as his word and asked the King to award him a commission. King Charles readily agreed and Richard was duly promoted to Ensign, the lowest officer rank in the King's Army. His new status was confirmed through an investiture in the Throne Room of the palace of Whitehall during which the King presented Richard with a parchment bearing the Seal Regnum, formally establishing his position as a commissioned officer in the service of the monarch. At the conclusion of the event, by way of celebration, Colonel Aston invited Richard to join him and his family for supper.

The Colonel had three daughters, ranging in age from nine to seventeen, and all were quite captivated by the handsome nineteen year old Ensign who had unexpectedly come to dine with them. Although the Colonel had decided, some time ago, not to be too inquisitive about the past of his young protégé, his daughters were not quite so reluctant to make enquiries.

"Where were you born Ensign Harfield and what brought you to London?" Sarah, the eldest of the Colonel's daughters, suddenly asked

"None of your business, Sarah," said her father abruptly, before adding a caution to anyone else who had thoughts of making enquiries of his guest. "I did not invite Ensign Harfield to supper to be interrogated by any of you three."

Richard was still a fugitive, but it was more than two years since he had found it necessary to flee from his home village of Prinsted and since he was now an officer in the King's Guard, and had established himself living under a new identity, he decided it would be safe to give at least a partial answer to Sarah's question. "I was born and spent my early years in a small village that lies some miles to the northwest of here. Soon after my father died, when I was sixteen, I decided to leave and seek my fortune here in London. Once arrived, however, I soon discovered that making even a very basic living here, let alone a fortune, is regrettably far from easy. Then a year ago I was caught up in an event which led me to meet the King and your father. Because of that chance encounter, I find myself fortunate enough to have been invited here tonight to dine in your most agreeable company."

Richard and Sarah remained gazing directly into each other's eyes until their mutual staring was eventually ended by the sound of the Colonel's voice. "It has been such a pleasant evening that I had quite lost track of the time. I see it is well past the girls' bedtime."

In order of age, with youngest first, as in a well drilled parade, aptly befitting the children of the Colonel of the King's Guard, the girls curtsied to their father, kissed him on the cheek and, with their mother leading the way, left the room to retire to bed. The last to leave was Sarah who was the only one to do other than bid Richard good night. She held out her hand which Richard took and kissed. "I hope we meet again soon Ensign Harfield," she said.

Then, out of sight of her father and to Richard's surprise, she gave him a wink.

Once the girls and their mother had left the room, the Colonel lit up a pipe and offered one to his guest. Richard declined the offer of the pipe, but accepted the brandy that was also offered.

"I have just learned more about you through your response to Sarah's question than I had discovered over the twelve months since we first met," said the Colonel. "Until tonight I only knew that you were the son of a man who was once a soldier in the service of King James. And, as I recall, you only volunteered that fact because I noticed King James' crest appears on the grip of your pistols and on your dagger's hilt. Is there anything else you are prepared to disclose, Richard? Remember, I am a man who owes you at least his livelihood, if not his life."

It had been more than three years since Richard's adoptive father had died and there had been someone in his life he trusted absolutely. As he considered how he should respond to the Colonel's question he recalled something that his father had said to him on more than one occasion. "If you wish to explore the true character of a man," Reverend Shuttleworth had said, "first look to see how he treats his family and how his family treats him." Richard had just witnessed how members of the Colonel's family interacted and taking this together with everything else he knew about the man, he felt sure that the Colonel was an honest and honourable man whom he could trust.

"My true name is Adam Wellings," he eventually said. "Both my parents died of the fever when I was just a few months old and I was adopted by the Prinsted village priest, Reverend Richard Shuttleworth. He was an elderly bachelor and the most kindly and honourable of men. I resided with him in the Vicarage until he died a little over three years ago. Very soon after his death a new priest arrived with his wife, to take his place. At first they appeared to treat me well and said I could continue to lodge free of charge at the Vicarage in exchange for carrying out a number of chores which I was happy to do. I also got occasional periods of paid employment at local farms, so I was able to maintain myself. However, after a few months the priest's attitude to me suddenly changed. He said that several items of church silver had gone missing and accused me of stealing them. I swore that I was innocent, but to no avail. I was arrested and things looked bad for me. The priest's wife claimed she had seen me remove the missing items from the Church and take them away in a bag. Everything they said about me was untrue and suddenly the real reason I had been allowed to remain at the Vicarage became clear. I was to take the blame for theft committed by the priest and his wife and to be flogged and imprisoned for their offences. If not hung! I knew I had little chance of being believed. What is the value of the word of a penniless orphan against the word of a priest and his wife? So, as soon as the opportunity for escape appeared, I took it and fled to London. I thought I might hide among the crowd and hopefully find some employment to keep from starving. I successfully achieved the first of those objectives, but, as you could see at our first meeting, Colonel, I was struggling to achieve the second."

Whilst sucking on his pipe and sipping his brandy, the Colonel had been listening attentively to Richard's story. Whilst its detail had previously been unknown to him, he was not surprised by its essence. "There is no man within the walls of this palace or its barracks who does not have some affair he wishes to keep secret. And I include myself and even the King himself in what I say, although I doubt His Majesty has any secrets of which I am unaware. As far as I am concerned, you are Ensign Richard Harfield, a brave and loyal soldier of King Charles and that is how you shall remain. Your secrets are as safe with me as are my own and those of His Majesty."

Richard smiled and gave a nod of appreciation, before making an enquiry of his own. "You have served with the King a very long time, have you not, sir?"

"Indeed I have," the Colonel replied, "ever since His Majesty was eleven years of age. His father appointed me as his son's chief bodyguard at the start of the troubles, almost twenty years ago, and I have been his principal protector ever since. Including, by the way, throughout the nine years he was forced to spend abroad, mostly in France. In fact, my youngest daughter, Lucy, was born there. All three of my girls speak French fluently and frequently chatter to one another in the language. Perhaps you would like to join in with their conversations from time to time to help maintain, and perhaps even improve, your own facility with the language?"

"I would very much like to do that, Sir," Richard responded. "But what of yourself, Colonel, do you speak much of the French language?"

The Colonel shook his head. "Regrettably, no, I do not. Not much at all. Despite living in France for the greater part of nine years during the King's exile, beyond learning a very basic vocabulary, I never applied myself sufficiently to acquire sound mastery of the language. During our time abroad there were numerous attempts on His Majesty's life carried out by Cromwell's agents. My time was almost exclusively taken up with countering those conspiracies and keeping the King safe and well. And that, let me tell you, was no straightforward undertaking. As you may well already have come to learn, His Majesty is a strong willed and free spirited individual. Having him compliant to any instruction, however reasonable, even when it was for his own good and meant to save his life, was no easy task. Yet somehow, and the Lord alone knows how, I managed to keep him alive. But there are times, even now, when I wish I had applied myself a little more rigorously to learning the French language. On command of the King, I still have to make occasional trips to France. Fortunately, I am invariably accompanied by His Majesty's French secretary, Monsieur Allard, who acts as my interpreter. In fact we will be paying our next short visit to France in a week's time."

At hearing this, a thought occurred to Richard. "I hope you will not think my request impertinent, Colonel, but would it be possible for me to accompany you on your French trip. I could act as your interpreter, which would relieve Monsieur Allard of the responsibility."

The Colonel smiled and topped up his own and Richard's brandy. "No, I do not see your request as impertinent, Richard. On the face of it, it would appear to be a most sensible suggestion. Monsieur Allard's absence from court and the King's side, even for a very brief period, always presents His Majesty with a few problems. But the mission that he and I are undertaking is not one where a simple substitution of the people involved can be made. Perhaps one day, maybe if you come to take over the office that I currently occupy, you will become privy to the purpose of these missions, but, for the time being, things must remain as they are."

Wednesday 1st July 1665

Very early in his career, Richard Harfield had proved himself to be a brave and loyal soldier of the King. Since becoming an officer he had also demonstrated his ability to lead and inspire other men. His reward had been quick promotion to the rank of Lieutenant and his establishment as Colonel Aston's most trusted aide and go-to officer of choice, when any potentially sensitive matter needed to be dealt with. One such matter had just arisen and the Colonel sent for Richard.

An outbreak of bubonic plague had been raging throughout London since February and the death toll was increasing daily. For many weeks past, the King's advisers had been trying to persuade him to leave the city and eventually their entreaties were successful.

"Tomorrow the King will move to Malmesbury House in Salisbury, together with certain members of the Court." said the Colonel. "I want you, Lieutenant Harfield, to take command of the guard that will accompany him. I am unable to attend myself because His Majesty has instructed me to go to France with Monsieur Allard. The number of men you take with you will be limited to fifty, since the King has agreed with the Lord Mayor that the greater part of the Regiment will remain in the city barracks, under the command of Major Beckwith, at least for the time being. The Mayor and Aldermen are concerned that the current disquiet and unrest amongst the people might turn to violence and they want the reassurance of having troops nearby. Monsieur Allard and I leave for France immediately after the King departs for Salisbury. God willing, we shall return within at most ten days and I shall then take my own family away from this noxious place. I would send them away now, but, regrettably, I have not had the opportunity to reserve suitable living quarters in Salisbury. I am hoping that you will undertake that task for me, Richard, in readiness for our arrival. The accommodation you select should be as close as possible to where the King will be residing and reasonably commodious. But I shall set no further restrictions upon it. Mine is a soldier's family and will cope with a measure of discomfort if needs be."

The sun was not yet up when the King, with a limited retinue, set out from Whitehall Palace. The early hour had been chosen deliberately, not only to avoid potential crowds, but also to reduce the risk of panic and despair taking hold, if the general populace were to witness their King leaving the capital.

Three weeks passed before the first news of Colonel Aston and Monsieur Allard was received in Salisbury, but it was not good. It reported only that the pair had not yet disembarked at Calais. Because of the plague that was raging in London, the French authorities had introduced quarantine measures. All ships arriving from England were required to remain off shore for forty days before disembarkation was allowed. But that wasn't the only bad news to be delivered. Reports concerning the progress of the plague in the capital were growing ever more alarming.

Richard was becoming increasingly concerned about the welfare of the Colonel's family and sought the King's permission to have them collected and brought to Salisbury. As the officer currently in charge of the King's bodyguard, it was impossible for Richard himself to go, so with the King's agreement, he dispatched two of his most trusted men on the ninety mile journey to London.

Four days later the men returned, but brought with them only the Colonel's youngest daughter, Lucy, and even more bad news. Sadly, since the Colonel left for France, his wife and two eldest daughters had all succumbed to the plague.

Not only did Richard feel deep sympathy for the Colonel, but also overwhelming grief on his own account. In the four years since first becoming acquainted with the Aston family, he had developed a great fondness for each of its members. In the case of Sarah, the Colonel's eldest daughter, an even deeper emotion had blossomed. He was also torn as he faced a terrible dilemma. Should he send a message to the Colonel, to arrive whilst he was perhaps still quarantined aboard his ship? Or should he do nothing, leaving the Colonel to discover the ill that had befallen his family upon his return to London, possibly many weeks hence? He pondered the matter for a while, before eventually deciding to send one of his men to deliver the sad news to the Colonel at the earliest opportunity.

Despite his best efforts, the messenger was unable to deliver Richard's message until late August, after the Colonel had already returned to England and was on his way back to London. Understandably, the Colonel was devastated by the news that greeted him, but took some small comfort from knowing that his youngest daughter, Lucy, had survived and was safe in Salisbury. Regardless of his personal feelings, however, he still had professional obligations to meet.

Travelling first to the Regiment's barracks in London to check on the state of his men, he was horrified to discover that a significant number were either dead or sick from the plague.

The Colonel's distress was made all the worse when he realised that his troops had needlessly remained in the city. The people had not indulged in riotous and violent behaviour, as the Mayor and Aldermen had feared, although this was due more to their dread of the plague, than the assuaging of any sense of grievance they may have felt. Despite his concern for his men the Colonel knew his overriding responsibility was to the King and quickly moved on to Salisbury, taking with him a number of the healthy and able bodied of his men. Still at some distance from the city, he made camp and sent a single envoy to give notice of his arrival.

Richard was overjoyed to hear of the Colonel's safe return and obtained the King's permission to go out and greet him. At their meeting the two men refrained from their normal handshake and stood several yards apart.

"Unless the King commands otherwise," said Colonel Aston, "I intend that my men and I shall remain here in camp for seven more days quarantine, before entering Salisbury. I have no wish that we should bring the pestilence into the city."

"I fear you are too late, Sir," said Richard. "The plague arrived here a few days ago. So far there have been seven deaths of which I am aware, but a number of others are sick. I have already started to make arrangements to have His Majesty move to Oxford, a place of which I have only heard good reports. But now that you are here, Sir, I shall await your orders."

"Carry on with your plan, Richard," said the Colonel. "I doubt I could come up with a better one. The safety and well being of the King must remain your paramount concern. But tell me about Lucy. Is she well?"

"Yes Sir, I am glad to say that she is in good health. The King provided quarters in his mansion and she is being well looked after. You have no concerns on that account. Have you any message that you wish me to convey to her?"

"Only that my affection for her grows ever stronger," the Colonel replied. "And that I shall endeavour to see her at the earliest opportunity, once I judge that it is safe to do so. But I also have a message for His Majesty. The Colonel stepped forward and placed a package on the ground. "I brought this from France. Give it to the King as soon as possible, but do not show it, or tell of it, to anyone else. Now return to the King. By the Grace of God we shall meet again soon."

Whilst waiting for his audience with the King, Richard examined the package he was to deliver. It was ordinary enough, although the Seal upon it was one with which he was unfamiliar and on its wrapping, written by an immature hand, almost certainly that of a child, there appeared just one word, 'Adeline'.

Sunday 6th September 1665

The bells of the city's churches were ringing out as the King and his entourage arrived in Oxford. Charles, perhaps understandably, thought it was his loyal subjects' way of welcoming him. But he was wrong. It was Sunday, and the bell ringers were giving thanks to God for another week ended without signs of the plague in their city. In fact, most of the inhabitants were entirely unaware of the King's arrival and may very well have been perturbed and even angered if they had been. He and his court were associated with London, where the plague continued to wreak havoc, and although he had been shielding in Salisbury for the past two months very few of the good citizens of Oxford were aware of this. Richard Harfield appreciated the situation well and in consequence had arranged for the King's entrance into the city to be a muted affair. Only a small group of the city's highest ranking citizens had been given prior notice of his arrival.

A few days after the King had settled into his new quarters, Colonel Aston brought an end to his self-imposed quarantine and came to join him in Oxford. This meant that Richard was no longer the senior officer carrying ultimate responsibility for the King's safety. In recognition of the loyal and effective service he had given during the Colonel's absence he was promoted to the rank of captain and granted a few days leave, the first for many months.

Colonel Aston was curious to know how the reclusive Richard Harfield intended to spend his leave time. He wondered if he would remain in his quarters reading books, as he had so often done when granted a period of leave in the past. Richard assured him that on this occasion he would not have time to read any books. There was a matter he had been meaning to deal with for some months, if not years, and now seemed to be a most appropriate time to tend to it.

Oxford was less than fifteen miles from Prinsted, the village where, as Adam Wellings, Richard had been born and spent his youth. It was also the place from where he had been forced to flee seven years earlier and, therefore, as far as he was concerned, a place of unfinished business.

Most things still looked very much the same to Richard as he rode into Prinsted. But one thing that was different was the recently painted sign that hung outside the village tavern bearing its new name, Cromwell's Treasure. Changing the tavern's name was something that many of the village folk had been itching to do for years, but until the ending of Cromwell's Protectorate and the restoration of the monarchy this had been impossible. Richard was aware of the name's significance to the village and the sight of it brought a smile to his face.

Dismounting outside the vicarage, Richard called to a young boy who was loitering nearby. "Bring clean water and feed for my horse," he said, throwing the lad a coin. "When I return, if he displays satisfaction with your efforts, you will receive another of those."

"What is your horse's name, sir?" asked the boy.

Richard gently patted his horse. "Gideon," he replied. "His name is Gideon."

Reverend Snook was alone in the vicarage parlour, sitting in a high backed chair, smoking a clay pipe and sipping red wine in front of a roaring fire. He had his back to the door and didn't bother to turn when Abigail, his maid, entered.

"Begging your pardon, Reverend," said Abigail, "but there's a young gentleman who wishes to speak with you. He says he's an old acquaintance."

"What's his name?" Snook asked abruptly.

"He wouldn't say, Reverend. He said he wanted it to be a surprise and that you'd recognise him straight away when you see him."

"You say he is a gentleman. Is that just his sex or is it also his quality that you refer to?" asked Snook, even more abruptly.

"Both, Reverend," Abigail replied. "He is very well dressed and clearly a gentleman of quality."

"Then show him in at once," Snook demanded.

Abigail curtsied, although Snook, still sitting with his back to her, would not have noticed.

Richard entered the parlour, closing the door behind him. "Thank you for agreeing to my request for an audience, Reverend Snook," he said. "It has been a long time since I last met with you and Mrs. Snook. I thought it was time we became reacquainted. I wonder if you still recognise me."

Snook turned towards his visitor, looked him up and down, but gave no sign of recognition. "Sadly my wife passed away four years ago," he said. "And my memory for faces is not what it used to be. These days I sometimes wonder if I would even recognise my own mother, God rest her soul. I regret to say I do not recollect you, sir. Who are you?"

"I am the man who you betrayed seven years ago," replied Richard, "and would have seen hang for crimes committed by you and your wife."

A look of recognition slowly came over Snook's face, only to be quickly replaced by an expression of sheer terror. He called out for his maid who, since she had been eavesdropping on the other side of the door, arrived instantly.

"Fetch Percy at once Abigail. And tell him to come armed," the distressed priest demanded.

"And tell him to bring his friends.......if he has any," Richard added with a grin.

Abigail, flustered, curtsied to both men before rushing out.

"What do you want of me?" asked the terrified Snook.

"Your life," Richard replied. "I have come to take your life."

Snook swallowed hard. "You mean to kill me?"

Richard responded with no hint of emotion. "There are many ways to take a man's life and only one of them involves killing. I intend that you shall suffer, just as you caused me to suffer seven years ago. You will go out into the world a penniless and homeless outcast, a pariah amongst men."

Snook began to recover some of his self-possession. "How do you plan on achieving your aim? I am a well respected man of God, an ordained priest and a man of standing in the community."

Richard smiled sardonically. "I prefer that I can make good on my intention, but my preference is marginal. If it happens that I am unsuccessful in my endeavour then I shall content myself with seeing you hang. Either way the matter will be concluded to my eventual satisfaction."

Snook's look of dread returned just as the parlour door burst open and three men rushed in, closely followed by Abigail. The men were armed with an assortment of agricultural implements. A pitchfork, a sickle, and an axe. Richard unholstered his two pistols, pointed them in the direction of the men and all three immediately froze.

"Which one of you is Percy?" Richard demanded.

"He is!" two of the men shouted out in unison, both pointing to the nervous looking third.

"You have good friends indeed," said Richard sarcastically, as he pointed a pistol at Percy's head. "But tell me, Percy, have you committed any grave sins since your last confession?"

A dumbstruck Percy said nothing in reply, but turned towards Abigail who instantly dropped her head to look at the floor.

Richard understood the body language. "The answer would appear to be, yes, it seems, Percy. So if I were to kill you now, I would be killing a man without absolution and you would go straight to hell. Would he not, Reverend Snook?"

Neither Percy nor Snook made any response.

"But you have nothing to fear from me, Percy, provided that you answer honestly the questions I am about to put to you," said Richard reassuringly. "Do you understand?"

Percy looked down the barrel of the pistol and nodded.

Richard responded with his own gentle nod of the head before continuing. "I am assuming that Reverend Snook is your employer, Percy. So, tell me, what kind of employer is he? Is he good natured and generous or, is he mean and cruel? Remember, Percy, only the truth will do. Your life depends on it."

Percy hesitated, but Abigail answered for him. "He is mean and cruel, sir. A thief. A hypocrite. And a defiler of innocent young virgins. He is no Christian and you will find nobody in this village who disagrees with me on that."

Snook began to protest, but was immediately silenced when, without turning to look at him, Richard pointed a pistol squarely at his head.

With Snook's objections suppressed, Richard returned to his interrogation of Percy. "What do you say, Percy? Does Abigail speak the truth?"

Percy said nothing but gave a nod of confirmation and, without prompting, so did his two companions.

"Well, given your clearly expressed views of Reverend Snook, I doubt that any one of you is prepared to die for him today," said Richard, as he re-holstered his pistols.

After instructing Percy's two companions to go about their business, Richard handed Percy two coins. "My horse, Gideon, is outside. Keep one of these coins for yourself and give the other to the boy who is minding him. Then take Gideon to the stables and see that his needs are tended to." Turning to Abigail, he added, "I shall be staying here for the night and will be sleeping in Reverend Snook's bed. Go and change the bed linen and then bring me some supper. Oh, and fetch me some of Reverend Snook's finest red wine."

After both servants had left to carry out their allotted chores, Richard unfurled a parchment he was carrying, laid it out on the table and instructed Snook to sign it.

"What is it?" Snook asked anxiously.

"It is a letter informing the Bishop of your decision to resign your Living here in Prinsted with immediate effect. And it further informs him that it is your Christian resolve to share out your entire wealth, such as it is, amongst your parishioners, by way of making some atonement for the evil you have done them during your incumbency. It also includes your confession of the wrong that you did me seven years ago. At exactly three o'clock tomorrow afternoon I shall deliver it to the Bishop on your behalf, giving you the time until then to flee."

"And what if I refuse to sign?" asked an even more anxious Snook.

"Then I shall immediately arrest you and take you straightaway to Oxford, where I will ensure that you are quickly tried and hanged within the week. Seven years ago, it was the word of you and your wife against mine alone. And I was just a penniless orphan, whilst you were a priest whose true character was still to be discovered. Today, I am an officer in the King's Guard, holding His Majesty's commission and also his favour. And, as we have both so recently heard, your true nature is now well understood by your parishioners. I have little doubt that a number of them will be keen to give their own testimony against you. Who now do you think will be believed?"

"For God's sake, sir, have mercy," Snook pleaded.

"I have shown you more mercy than you deserve, or that you ever showed to me," said Richard. "I have given you your options. Either you sign this letter and have the opportunity to flee, with a chance to save your life or you will be taken to Oxford, where you will be tried and hanged within the week. Which is it to be?"

Snook realising the hopelessness of his situation, picked up his quill and signed Richard's parchment. "What now?" he asked.

Richard ordered Snook out into the vicarage's entrance hall where he gave him his instructions. "You will leave Prinsted at once, never to return. And I advise you to travel as far away as you can, as quickly as you can. Once I deliver your letter to the Bishop you will be publicly branded an outlaw and a bounty will be placed on your head. Exactly as happened to me seven years ago. You may also wish to pray that we never meet again because, if we do, I shall not hesitate to kill you and claim the bounty myself."

Snook put on his boots, coat and hat. "Can I take some money?" he asked, still struggling to come to terms with his sudden change of fortune.

Richard threw him a silver sixpence. "That's half a shilling more than I had with me when I was forced to flee from here. You are indeed a lucky man."

Snook caught the sixpence, opened the door and walked out into the night.

Having returned to the parlour, Richard didn't have to wait long before Abigail delivered his supper, together with a carafe of red wine. "I saw the Reverend leaving," she said. "Will he be returning later?"

"No," Richard replied. "He will not be returning tonight or, indeed, at any time in the future. But I doubt it will be too long before a new priest arrives to take his place and become your new employer. Until that happens though, we must locate some funds to provide for you and Percy. Where does Reverend Snook keep his treasure?"

Abigail was shocked by Richard's question and took time deciding how to respond. "I really cannot say, sir," she eventually replied.

Richard was not convinced. "Is that cannot, or will not? I know little, if anything, of the workings of a woman's mind, but I know that few secrets can be kept from a nosy eavesdropping housemaid, especially one as pretty and clever as you. So, I shall repeat my question, Abigail. Where does Reverend Snook keep his treasure?"

Unsure whether she should take Richard's words as a reprimand or a compliment, Abigail took a moment to consider before eventually deciding on the latter. "I'm not certain, sir," she replied. "All I know is that after he'd counted the Sunday collection he would immediately take the money up to his bedroom. And whenever he needed to make a payment, that's where he brought the money from. But where he kept it hidden in there, I don't know."

Richard smiled broadly. "And not for want of you searching for it, I'll warrant, eh, Abigail? But, no matter, if his treasure is hidden somewhere in his bedroom, I shall find it."

After supper Richard retired to Reverend Snook's bedroom. It was the room in which Reverend Shuttleworth, Richard's adoptive father, had once slept and, where, as a child, he himself had often played. Most things appeared just as he remembered them. Neither the furniture nor even the pictures on the wall had been changed since he left. Only the carpet on the floor was new. In his father's time there had been no carpet, just bare floorboards that creaked when they were walked on and sometimes even when they weren't. One loose floorboard had been especially noisy and he had named it 'Old Rowdy', but Shuttleworth had always refused to fix it. He said it was the alarm that would wake him if a thief were ever to enter his bedroom in the night. Richard knew this to be only partially true, because on the one occasion he had lifted 'Old Rowdy' he discovered that his father had hidden some of the church silver in the space beneath. Now, years later, after pulling back the carpet, he was pleased to find that 'Old Rowdy' had neither been replaced nor secured. He lifted it, and smiled.

The next morning, before leaving Prinsted, Richard called at the home of Dr. Alexander de Calvairac, the village leech.

De Calvairac and his family, protestant Huguenot refugees from Catholic France, had arrived in Prinsted some years before Richard was born. He soon became a close friend of Richard's adoptive father, the Reverend Shuttleworth, and a man in whom the priest placed great trust. Richard, whilst still known as Adam Wellings was also to become a close friend of de Calvairac's grandson, Robert.

Although de Calvairac was already a man of advanced years when Richard last saw him seven years earlier, remembering him as being a particularly healthy and rugged specimen, he thought there was a good chance the old man might still be alive. As it turned out, he was.

The door of de Calvairac's cottage was opened by his housekeeper, Chastity Weston. Richard introduced himself as Captain Harfield of the King's Guards Regiment and said he wished to speak with her master on a confidential matter of great importance. Suitably impressed, the housekeeper led him through to the garden at the rear of the cottage where de Calvairac was tending to his beehives.

At the best of times the old man's eyesight was poor. Without his spectacles and with a finely meshed veil trailing down from his apiarist's hat and wafting in the breeze, there was little chance he was going to instantly recognise Richard, especially since he had not seen him for more than seven years.

Richard began the explanation for his visit by placing a small wooden chest on the garden table, opening the lid and inviting de Calvairac to inspect its contents.

The old man stepped forward, raised his veil and looked inside the box. Then, just to make sure that his imperfect eyesight was not deceiving him, he ran his fingers through the many coins and pieces of jewellery the box contained. "Where did this come from?" he asked. "And what has it to do with me?"

"It comes from a benefactor who wishes it to be shared out amongst the good folk of Prinsted," Richard replied. "And I have come to ask if you will agree to take on the task of ensuring that it is honestly and fairly distributed. What do you say?"

De Calvairac was understandably taken aback by this most unexpected revelation and took some time to gather his thoughts. "And who is this most generous benefactor?" he eventually asked.

"The Reverend Snook," Richard replied.

"Snook!" exclaimed the incredulous Frenchman, before bursting out laughing. "Now I know that you jest. That scoundrel would not bestow his piss on a burning man, let alone donate such treasure as this."

Richard handed over the parchment that Snook had signed the previous evening. "This document proves that I speak the truth. It is Snook's confession to having committed numerous sins against the people of Prinsted during his tenure here, and his wish to atone, through gifting them his entire wealth. I intend delivering the document to the Bishop later today."

De Calvairac removed his beekeeper's hat, put on his spectacles and read through Snook's letter. Conceding that it appeared to confirm everything he had just been told he handed it back to Richard, but did not immediately let go of it. For several seconds, and without saying a word, he continued to hold on to the parchment, whilst staring directly into Richard's eyes. Eventually he released his grip and spoke. "I sense we may have had some previous acquaintanceship, Captain, although, for the life of me, I cannot recall where or when. It is indeed the oddest feeling that I have. And I am intrigued to know why you chose to come to me with this commission."

"I have come to you, because I know you to be the most highly respected member of this community, someone whom the villagers will trust to be both fair and just. Given the profession that you have so diligently practiced these many long years, it is also unlikely there is anyone residing in the parish with whom you are not acquainted, or of whose circumstances you are unaware. In short, sir, you are the ideal choice. As for the possibility of the two of us having had some previous acquaintanceship, I can confirm that we most certainly have. It lasted for sixteen years, ending a little over seven years ago, when I was forced to flee for my life, because of lies told by Snook and his wife. You knew me as Adam Wellings, adopted son of your friend, Reverend Shuttleworth."

Understandably shocked by this disclosure de Calvairac took a moment for the news to sink in. When eventually it did, he placed his hands on Richard's shoulders. "Praise the Lord," he said. "I believed you to be long since dead. But now I see that is as far from the truth as it is possible to be. And I am overjoyed at the discovery." The old man took a step back and looked Richard up and down. "If only your father could see you now! How proud he would be. It was indeed a dark day when Snook and his wife accused you of stealing the Church silver. I, myself, found it impossible to believe, but because of the prestige that went with Snook's office, many in the village and those in authority were persuaded. If the situation were to be repeated today though, the outcome would surely be different. So many in this parish can now bear witness to the devious, immoral and ungodly actions of the Reverend Snook. Indeed, it is only their superstition regarding the eternal damnation they fear he can bring down upon them, that has prevented them from denouncing him and allowed him to retain his position these last few years."

"Well the people need fear his malediction no more," said Richard. "Snook removed himself from Prinsted yesterday evening, never to return. And he left with only the clothes he was wearing and a single sixpence to ease his way. Later today, he will be declared an outlaw and a bounty put on his head. The Church does not react kindly to those who admit to stealing its treasures. I doubt he will survive the month."

"And what of you?" asked de Calvairac. "What is written on that parchment will clear your name. Will you now return to being Adam Wellings, or will you continue as Richard Harfield?"

"Had my name been cleared some years ago then I would have been quick to reclaim it," Richard replied. "But much time has now passed and I am no longer that person. I was born Adam Wellings, but I shall die Richard Harfield. I trust you will keep my secret."

The old man smiled and patted Richard on the arm. "You can be sure of it. And, as the Good Lord is my witness, I shall do my best to ensure Snook's endowment is fairly and equitably distributed throughout the parish."

Wednesday 29th May 1680:
King Charles II's Fiftieth Birthday

It was twenty years since Adam Wellings saved the life of the King and took the name Richard Harfield. Ever since that time he had served as a brave and loyal member of the King's Guards Regiment and been responsible for preserving the King's life on a number of further occasions. His faithful service and outstanding leadership skills had not gone unnoticed. By the time of the King's fiftieth birthday he had risen to the rank of major and stood second only to Colonel Aston in the King's favour.

The King began his fiftieth birthday celebrations by giving brief audiences to numerous visiting emissaries, both domestic and foreign, who arrived at the Court of St James to deliver gifts and express their good wishes. The festivities that followed went on into the early hours of the following morning, only ending when the King eventually decided to call a halt to the merrymaking and retired to his private apartment. Colonel Aston and Major Harfield had been at the King's side throughout the day and evening and were far from unhappy when the last of the guests departed.

Colonel Aston slumped into a well cushioned chair. "My legs and indeed every other part of my body have today reminded me, and not for the first time, that I am no longer a young man, Richard. These unwelcome prompts have recently begun to affront me with ever increasing frequency, compelling me to acknowledge a particular inevitability.

In two months I shall be sixty-five and I have decided that it is an appropriate age for me to begin my transformation from soldier to gentleman-at-leisure. I have already raised the subject of my retirement with His Majesty. In fact our discussions on the matter are well advanced and we have already agreed on who my successor should be."

Until that moment Richard had never given even a moment's thought to the Colonel retiring and was shocked at hearing this completely unexpected announcement. Quickly thinking through its potential implications, one in particular gave him cause for concern. "Will your successor be Major Beckwith, sir?" he asked, with obvious apprehension.

"Good God, no!" exclaimed Colonel Aston. "If Beckwith were to become responsible for the safety of the King, His Majesty would be dead within the week. Beckwith is barely excusable as an aide-de-camp and certainly no leader of men. He only got commissioned into the Regiment and raised to his current rank, because he's the fourth son of a wealthy nobleman who once paid off His Majesty's gambling debts. It is you, Richard, who will take over as Colonel of the Regiment upon my retirement. The King and I are both settled on it. So what do you say?"

Richard was genuinely surprised. "I am extremely honoured Colonel, but you have just made two quite unexpected announcements. I think I need more time to fully come to terms with their implications."

"And you shall have it," Colonel Aston responded. "My birthday is eight weeks hence. We have until then to prepare you fully to take over the position that I currently occupy.

And the process of transition will start almost immediately. First get some rest and then later today, at noon, join me, Monsieur Allard and the King, in His Majesty's private apartment. We have an important matter to discuss with you."

Thursday 30th May 1680

The clock was striking twelve noon as Richard and Colonel Aston entered into the King's private drawing room. Apart from the King himself the only other person present was Monsieur Allard, his private secretary.

The King began by confirming that Richard would be promoted to the rank of Colonel and take over command of the King's Guards Regiment when Colonel Aston retired, but this was not the only subject he wished to discuss. "I have in mind a commission that in the past I would have entrusted to Colonel Aston but, since you will soon take over his office, it would seem appropriate to hand responsibility for the matter to you, Major Harfield. It is an assignment of the utmost sensitivity. What I am about to tell you must be treated with your greatest discretion and no part of it should ever be repeated, except for those few details that are necessarily communicated to ensure the enterprise is brought to a successful conclusion."

Richard gave the necessary assurances and the King continued. "Over many generations, Bollezeele, a large and prosperous village in north east France, has been home to the de la Vallée family. The last born and, I regret to say, now the sole remaining member of that family, is the young granddaughter of a couple who, for a period of several months during my enforced absence from England, gave me shelter and protection. Since her birth, the young woman has resided with her grandparents at their home in Bollezeele. However, word has lately reached me that both have recently died, leaving her alone and in need of support. I intend to repay her grandparents' many kindnesses to me by taking her under my protection. Therefore, Major Harfield, I command that you go to Bollezeele and fetch her here to England, where I can best provide for her. I understand that the young woman speaks little English, but I am aware that you have some facility with the French language and therefore should have no difficulty with communication. In any case, Colonel Aston has agreed that his daughter, Lucy, will accompany you to serve as the young woman's companion and, when required, act as her interpreter. Lucy will continue in that role for some months after your return to England, during which time she will assist the young woman in becoming fluent in English and familiar with our customs."

"Monsieur Allard and Colonel Aston will provide you with all further details you may require, including the address where the young woman is to be accommodated here in England. Ordinarily I would ask Monsieur Allard to accompany you, but his services are needed here making arrangements for the young woman's arrival, ensuring her new home is appropriately staffed and equipped to satisfy the requirements of a lady living under the protection of the King. My final statement on the matter, Major Harfield, is that you should afford the same level of protection to the woman as you would to me."

At the conclusion of his briefing, completed by Colonel Aston and Monsieur Allard, Richard was handed a plain sealed envelope.

"Give this to the young woman when you arrive at her home in Bollezeele," said Monsieur Allard. "The letter it contains explains everything she needs to know and makes it clear that she can trust you. It must be given only to her. Do not open the envelope yourself and do not let anyone else know of its existence. Finally, and most importantly, at no time should you make any mention of the King's interest in this matter. Not to her, or to anyone else. Since childhood the woman has been aware that she and her family have received numerous benefits due to her grandparents' close friendship with a high ranking member of English society, but that is all she knows. She is entirely unaware that her family's longstanding and generous benefactor is the King himself. At some time, after she is brought safely to England, perhaps it will be appropriate to tell her more, but that is a matter on which His Majesty will decide."

"And the woman's name?" asked Richard.

"Adeline," replied the Colonel. "The woman's name is Adeline."

Monday 3rd June 1680

The detailed instructions provided by Monsieur Allard and the Colonel meant that Richard, accompanied by Lucy, had no difficulty navigating his way to Bollezeele and to the home of the de la Vallée family. It was certainly the largest house in the village, but turned out to be far less grand than Richard had imagined it would be. Especially since it had once been, albeit for a relatively short time, home to the King.

It was late morning when Richard and Lucy rode into the courtyard and it would have been reasonable to assume that a house servant, or possibly even Adeline herself, would have come out to greet them. As it was, even after Richard had knocked on the door a number of times and several minutes had passed, no one appeared.

"Where is everyone?" Richard asked rhetorically. "Have we arrived on some saint's feast day? Is everyone at church?"

Lucy responded only with a shrug, before suddenly calling out and pointing to one of the first floor windows. "Up there! I saw someone. It was only fleeting, but I'm certain I didn't imagine it."

Richard looked up at the window and called out Adeline's name several times. Then holding aloft the envelope that Monsieur Allard had given him he announced in French that he had arrived from England carrying a message from an old friend of her grandparents, someone who was offering her his help and protection. After placing the envelope on the doorstep he moved back twenty paces, hoping for a reaction. Several minutes elapsed before the door opened slightly, just wide enough and long enough for a hand to reach out and pick up the envelope, before it was once more slammed shut.

Several more minutes passed before the door was once again unlocked, but this time it was opened fully and a beautiful young woman stepped out. It had been fourteen years since Colonel Aston's eldest daughter, Sarah, had died from the plague leaving a great void in Richard's heart. At his first site of Adeline, the void began to fill.

As Richard and Lucy entered the manor house they were both immediately struck by its generally threadbare state and its sparse furnishing. Their surprise showed in their faces, prompting Adeline to explain the reasons for the circumstances in which they found her.

Some years before she was born, Adeline's maternal grandfather had made several disastrous investments. One speculative bout in the late sixteen thirties had turned out to be especially ruinous. He had invested heavily in the Dutch tulip bulb market, only to see prices almost immediately crash and practically the whole of his fortune wiped out overnight. After that particular episode the family had had to sell all their treasured heirlooms and valuable furniture, piece by piece, just in order to make ends meet. Fortunately, however, when the point was reached where there was nothing of any value left to sell, apart from the family home itself, and destitution seemed imminent, salvation arrived.

The year before Adeline was born a wealthy young Englishman arrived at the mansion and stayed lodging there for several months. Ever since that time he had remained the family's benefactor. And twice each year his envoys would arrive to deliver money and gifts. Adeline had never met the man and did not know his identity, but she realised it must be the same man who was now offering her a home and his protection in England. She went on to describe how, since the death of her grandparents several months earlier, her circumstances had deteriorated significantly. Having been left with barely enough money to pay for their funerals, she discovered there were a number of debts outstanding. Debts she could not repay. Any day now, her grandfather's creditors would arrive to claim the house as payment and she would be turned out, destitute. It appeared that her family's English benefactor had come to her aid at just the right moment. Her father, she said, had died before she was born and her mother had died giving birth to her. With her grandparents also now dead there was nothing to hold her in Bollezeele and she was grateful to accept her benefactor's kind and generous offer.

Adeline placed her letter on the table and, accompanied by Lucy, went to pack up her few personal belongings. Richard had been instructed not to open the envelope he had delivered, but he had not been told he could not read its contents. Bearing Monsieur Allard's personal seal, the letter was extremely brief. It stated only that Adeline's English benefactor was offering her a home and his protection, and that if she wished to accept then she should return to England with the two people who delivered it.

By mid afternoon, two large trunks, each bearing the de la Vallée Coat of Arms, had been loaded onto an old wagon to which Lucy's horse had been hitched. Adeline went round the house closing up all the window shutters and locking all the doors, internal and external, before finally exiting through the door that led into the courtyard where Richard and Lucy were waiting. It was the house in which she had been born and until this day lived her entire life. She took a moment to reflect on the many happy years she had spent there, before mounting the cart alongside Lucy.

As they drove out of the courtyard Adeline threw the key ring down the well.

Tuesday 3rd June 1681

In the twelve months since arriving in England, Adeline had been residing in a small manor house in the village of Scottern, a few miles to the north west of London. The property had been especially purchased for her by the King, although she was unaware of this. In fact, Adeline knew nothing of the King's involvement in her life. She knew only that the house had been provided by the unidentified wealthy Englishman who had been her generous benefactor ever since the time of her birth.

It was originally intended that Lucy would remain with Adeline only until her services as language and cultural tutor were no longer required, but because of the strong bond of friendship that had developed between them the King agreed that Lucy could stay on indefinitely, acting as Adeline's companion and chaperone.

Monsieur Allard had personally chosen and appointed a small group of servants to the household, although since Adeline had taken up residence he had rarely visited. On the other hand, Richard, who had recruited a trio of recently retired ex-Royal Guardsmen to provide security for the property, was a frequent visitor. And it grew increasingly obvious why.

Today was special. It was exactly one year since Richard's first meeting with Adeline and he planned on paying her a visit to ask her a most important question. It was a question to which her answer would determine the course of the rest of their lives. He was preparing to set off, when a message arrived from Colonel Aston saying that he needed to see him as soon as possible on a most urgent matter.

Following Colonel Aston's retirement, almost one year earlier, the King had offered him a grace-and-favour apartment in St James' Palace. The Colonel, however, had graciously declined the offer, preferring instead to settle in a cottage in the neighbouring village to where Adeline and Lucy, his only surviving daughter, both resided. With very little inconvenience, therefore, Richard was able to respond to the Colonel's urgent summons by calling to see him on his way to visit Adeline. When he arrived he found the Colonel sitting in his garden, drinking lemonade.

The two men greeted one another as the old friends they were and Colonel Aston asked Richard if he knew much about butterflies.

Richard shook his head. "No, Sir, it is not a subject of which I have even the most limited knowledge. Do you?"

"I didn't used to, but lately I have begun to take an interest," the Colonel replied. "Since retiring and spending so much of my time in my garden, I have found it hard to ignore them. Take that one over there, for instance." The Colonel pointed to a black and orange butterfly perched on a rose petal a few feet away. "That is a Monarch Butterfly. I've been wondering how it got its name. Perhaps it is free-spirited and headstrong, rather like our own dear monarch! But who knows?"

Richard had no wish to appear rude, but he was eager for the Colonel to explain the reason for his summons.

He wanted to take his leave and be on his way to meet with Adeline as soon as possible. "Please forgive my bluntness, Colonel, but I doubt you invited me to an urgent meeting in order to discuss the wildlife in your garden."

The Colonel smiled. "No, quite right, Richard, and with equal bluntness I shall come straight to the point. Lucy tells me that your relationship with Adeline has developed to such a degree that you intend making a proposal of marriage imminently, and that Adeline is almost certain to give you a positive response. Is that correct?"

Richard was both surprised and vexed by the Colonel's question. "There is nobody in this world that I hold in higher esteem than you, Sir. And I would willingly answer, honestly, almost any question that you might care to ask of me, but you have no business asking me that one. It appears that Lucy has been discussing my personal affairs without my approval, or even my knowledge, and I am deeply offended at the thought of it."

"Please don't judge Lucy too harshly," said the Colonel. "Whatever she has said to me has its roots in the affection in which she holds you and, of course, Adeline. And, as for my intrusion into your personal affairs, ordinarily I would entirely agree with you. But what you are planning cannot be considered an entirely personal affair. There is the King's opinion on the matter to be considered. Have you given any thought to that? Although Adeline is currently unaware of it, the King has been her life-long benefactor and, more recently, also become her guardian. Does that not entitle His Majesty to have some say on the subject?"

"I don't see why the King's opinion on the matter should be of any consequence," Richard objected. "It is true that

Adeline has been living under his protection and that he has provided for her most generously during these past twelve months, but after we are married that will come to an end. As her husband, it will be my responsibility to provide for her and I have the resources and income to do that most adequately. I intend to inform His Majesty of my plans after I have made my proposal to Adeline and she has accepted. But I shall be doing it only as a courtesy, not to seek his opinion on the matter, let alone his permission. Both Adeline and I are passed the age of majority and therefore entirely free to decide our future for ourselves. If Adeline's father was alive I would, of course, first approach him and ask his permission to marry his daughter, but I shall grant that privilege to no one else, not even to the King"

"So, if Adeline's father was alive, you would speak with him first, before making your proposal to her?" asked the Colonel, seeking confirmation of what he had just heard.

"Indeed I would," Richard replied. "It would be the correct thing to do."

"Then you must speak with the King urgently on the matter!" the Colonel exclaimed abruptly.

"Why?" asked a puzzled Richard, with equal abruptness.

The Colonel grew red in the face and raised his arms to the heavens. "Damn it, Richard, because she is his child!"

The two men sat in silence for several minutes, during which time the Colonel's colouring returned to its normal hue and Richard was able to slowly recover from the shock of what he had just heard. "So, Adeline is yet another of the King's many bastards!" he said.

"No, she is not," responded the Colonel, "although life for all of us, including her, might be much easier if she were. Adeline is the one and only legitimate child of His Majesty and, therefore, heir to the throne of England."

Richard was still coming to terms with this second revelation as the Colonel began to explain. "At all times during the King's forced exile his life was under threat from Cromwell's agents, but there was one period when the situation became particularly hazardous. Not long before his death, Cromwell flooded the continent with his spies and would-be assassins, and placed a substantial bounty on the King's head. There were potential informers everywhere and no place was judged to be even remotely safe. It was then that Monsieur Allard made a proposal. He had a distant cousin, a member of the French gentry, but one who had lately fallen on hard times and was having difficulty making ends meet. The cousin, who Allard described as a pious and honourable man, lived with his wife and daughter in a modest mansion in the village of Bollezeele, but, because of the family's financial circumstances, there were no servants. In exchange for a small allowance the family gave sanctuary to the King until the threat and menace that he faced eased. Apart from the family themselves, only Monsieur Allard and I ever knew where His Majesty had taken refuge. The fact there were no servants employed at the property made his situation all the more secure, albeit rather less luxurious than His Majesty might have wished. It was a strategy of secrecy and seclusion that we employed and fortunately it worked."

"The King resided with the family for about six months during which time he managed to fall in love with the daughter of the household. So deeply did he fall, in fact, that he made a proposal of marriage, which she accepted. The family, who were all devout Catholics, arranged a private marriage ceremony in the village church. Apart from the village priest and the bride and groom, only four other people were present to witness the event: the bride's parents; Monsieur Allard; and, me. Little more than a month later, to the great joy of the King, his wife announced that she was with child. Not long after the King had arrived in Bollezeele, Oliver Cromwell died and his son, Richard, was appointed Lord Protector in his place. Richard was a weak and foolish man and quickly lost all authority. Agents that his father had sent out to hunt down the King returned to England and informers went unpaid, so lost interest in the pursuit. The situation began to change dramatically and it grew increasingly clear that the King would soon be restored to his throne. It was then possible for him to leave Bollezeele, but it was decided that his wife should remain with her parents until after the birth of her child. It was intended that once the King was restored to his throne, his wife and child would come to England to join him. Sadly, that was never to be. Within a few hours of giving birth to Adeline, the King's wife was dead."

"But why did the King leave Adeline with her grandparents for all those years?" asked Richard. "Why didn't he publicly acknowledge her and have her brought to England as a child, once he had been restored to the throne?"

"Politics!" replied the Colonel. "But I have said enough. If you are to learn anymore then it must come from the lips of His Majesty. After what I have told you, I assume that you will now agree to speak with him, before making your proposal to Adeline?"

Richard nodded. "There appears to be no alternative. I shall seek a private audience with him later today."

"No, leave it until tomorrow," the Colonel demanded. "It is important that I speak to the King before you do. He needs to know about our conversation and must be forewarned of what you now know. I myself shall go and see him later today. And there is one final detail which you must at all times keep in mind. Adeline has absolutely no knowledge of what I have just told you and, until the King commands otherwise, that is how it must remain."

Although Richard remained eager to see Adeline, after what he had just heard, he thought better of it and returned to his quarters at Whitehall Palace.

Wednesday 4th June 1681

The King was alone and seated on his throne in the elaborately decorated Throne Room of St James' Palace when Richard arrived for their private meeting.

"I thought that holding our discussion amidst this grandeur would serve as a reminder of my dignity, power and majesty," said the King.

"I need no reminder of it, Sir," Richard responded.

Charles rose up from the throne and stepped down from the dais on which it stood. "Perhaps not," he said. "However, there are occasions when I find that I do. But despite all of this extravagant and glorious display, and the prestige that attaches to my person and position, it would appear that you and I have much in common."

Richard was doubtful. "I struggle to see that, Sir."

The King placed a hand on Richard's shoulder. "Do we not both know what it is to be a hunted man, Richard? Not knowing whom to trust, or if we will survive another night alive."

Richard was taken by surprise. "You know of my circumstances before we first met, Sir?"

"Indeed I do," the King replied. "And have done since the very beginning. It was obvious to me at our first meeting that you were a fugitive, although from who or what, I did not know. But then yesterday, Colonel Aston explained it all to me. Fair and wise man that he is, he decided that if you were to know my deepest secrets then I should know yours. He also informed me that you have inflicted a just punishment on those who treated you cruelly, something else we have in common. But there is more, much more. In particular, I have just discovered that we feel love for the same woman, although in my case it is the love of a father, not a suitor. Colonel Aston tells me you are curious as to why I have not publicly proclaimed Adeline as my legitimate daughter and heir but chosen to keep her hidden away all these years, ignorant of her true identity and rank. Your curiosity is understandable and no doubt all the greater, having just heard me profess my love for her. Let me begin the appeasement of your curiosity by asking you a question, Richard. What is it that holds my kingdom together, when there are so many conflicting forces that seek to tear it apart, religion being first amongst them?"

"You," Richard replied. "It is Your Majesty who keeps the country united."

The King shook his head. "If only that were true, Richard! If it were, then I would have proclaimed Adeline from the day of her birth. But, alas, it is not the figure of the King alone that unites this great country. It is good politics that prevents disharmony, fragmentation and strife from taking hold, before eventually driving the nation into civil war. Sadly, that is something my dear father, God rest his soul, forgot. Assuming he ever knew it in the first place, which I doubt."

"The life of a King is not his own, Richard. And as soon as he begins to think it might be, he is doomed. That is something else my father failed to understand. However, there was one brief period when, for a fleeting moment, I lived as if I did have command of my own destiny. The short time I spent in Bollezeele was the happiest of my life. Although I knew my enemies could arrive and bring it to an end at any instant, I cared not, for I had found true love, just as you appear to have done. But then it all ended, just as suddenly as it had begun. The love of my life was dead and I was once more thrust back into the cage of responsibility. My life was no longer my own, nor would it ever be again. In the beginning, the decisions I took regarding Adeline were easy to make. England was still not entirely settled and I had no desire to put my child in harm's way. But then a much harder question arose. Adeline's mother was a devout Catholic, as were both her parents. When we married I swore an oath to raise as a good Catholic any child we might be blessed with. Perhaps you can already see my dilemma, Richard. Was this kingdom ready to accept a Catholic girl child, whose mother was a French commoner, as heir to the throne? Twenty years ago the answer to that question was definitely no! And it still is. You will remember that nine years ago I made a Royal Declaration of Indulgence, intended to extend religious liberty to Catholics, but, within months, Parliament compelled me to withdraw it. I had hoped that over time, the enmity felt towards Catholicism in this country might diminish, but sadly, quite to the contrary, it has increased. Lately we have had the allegation of a Popish Plot put about by the liar Titus Oates, resulting in innocent Catholics being executed and false accusations made even against the Queen. The ease with which such slanders came to be generally believed clearly illustrates the depth of hostility that still exists towards Catholics in this country. Would any father wish to risk introducing his daughter into such an unhappy domain? I think not. Apart from Monsieur Allard and Colonel Aston, you are the only other living person who is aware of Adeline's true identity, and I pray to God that it stays that way. Her security and happiness are far more important to me than the thought that she should succeed me on the throne."

"With Adeline unacknowledged, Your Majesty, then it is your brother, James, who currently stands as your heir. And he too is widely believed to be a Catholic," said Richard.

The King nodded. "Indeed he is, although I have forbidden him from making a public display or declaration of his faith. If it does come to pass that he succeeds me on the throne then he will be free to do as he pleases, but he will be well advised to keep his true religious beliefs a wholly private matter. This realm is not prepared to accept a Catholic as its monarch and nor will it be for many years to come. If ever."

"So, what of Adeline your Majesty?" asked Richard.

"Adeline will never inherit my throne," replied the King. "If she did, then I doubt that even you could save her, Richard. That is a decision that I took for both of us a long time ago and we have each had to live with its consequences. Not a day has gone by when I have not thought of her, although in her entire life I have never cast eyes upon her, nor she upon me. But as to your original purpose in coming to see me, that is a different matter. I was once a man who married for love. I would surely be a hypocrite of the worst kind if I denied my own child that same liberty. And I have always considered hypocrisy to be the most iniquitous of sins. Adeline will marry who she pleases and I am reliably informed that her heart is set on you. Awareness of that fact has prompted me to make a number of decisions that I have hitherto rather wantonly postponed. Although the day when Adeline learns of her true relationship to me is still some time off, I have decided that the time has come when she shall learn the identity of her hitherto unknown benefactor. Indeed, I am most confidently advised that she has already expressed her suspicions that it must be a royal prince of the House of Stuart, although she does not yet appear to have fixed her mind firmly on me. Accordingly, I have instructed Monsieur Allard to pay her a visit this morning to inform her. At the same time he will stress upon her the necessity of treating the intelligence as an entirely confidential matter. I have also commissioned Sir Godfrey Kneller to paint her portrait and he will be travelling to Scottern later today to begin working on it.

The King picked up a small jewellery box from a side table and handed it to Richard. "This contains the jewellery that my mother wore on the day she married my father. It is my engagement gift to Adeline. Nothing would give me greater pleasure than if she were to wear it on the occasion of her own wedding. I will be extremely grateful if you could also persuade her to wear the rubies whilst she is sitting for Sir Godfrey. I have already informed him of the various other features that I wish to see included in the portrait, whilst making it clear that my involvement in the matter must not be discussed with anyone, except for you and Adeline herself. When the portrait is completed I intend to hang it in my private apartment where I can look on it each day."

"Will there ever come a time when you will tell Adeline her true relationship to you Your Majesty?" Richard asked.

"Perhaps," the King replied, ruefully. "We shall see what the future holds, but for the time being things must remain essentially as they are. However, there is one detail that I am well minded to change. I am determined that no daughter of mine shall marry a man without a title. You entered this room as Colonel Richard Harfield. You shall leave as Colonel, Sir Richard, First Baronet Harfield."

At the conclusion of his meeting with the King, Richard immediately went to visit Adeline in Scottern. Sir Godfrey Kneller and two of his assistants had arrived before him and were already busy in the main drawing room preparing for Adeline's first sitting. Adeline herself was not yet present, so, in the hope that his plans had not been entirely thwarted, Richard went looking for her. When he found her he instantly dropped down on one knee and, in time honoured fashion, made his proposal of marriage, which she immediately accepted. It was all done more hurriedly than Richard would have preferred, but it meant he could then legitimately present Adeline with the engagement gift from her benefactor and request that she wear it during her portrait sitting, just as the King had asked.

Richard had witnessed Sir Godfrey Kneller at work around the Court on several previous occasions. He was quite familiar with his style of operation and well acquainted with the portrait artist's deliberate and studied inclusion of carefully chosen items of symbolic meaning in his paintings. On entering the drawing room with Adeline, he was therefore surprised to see one particular item mounted on the wall in the background of the scene that was to be painted. He took Sir Godfrey to one side to discuss it.

"What do you mean by having an image of the King in this portrait?" Richard asked.

Sir Godfrey was startled by Richard's tone. "The King himself instructed me to include it," he said. "It is a portrait of His Majesty seated on St Edward's Chair that I myself painted shortly after his coronation. Why he wants it to appear in this particular portrait, I know not. But who am I, or you, to question the King's resolve?"

Friday 12th September 1681

The bells of St Joseph's, the village church at Scottern, rang out loudly on the morning of the marriage between Richard and Adeline. And as the time when the bride was expected to make her appearance drew near, there remained very few vacant seats on the right hand side of the church. This was understandable, since the overwhelming majority of those present to witness the event were either friends or comrades-in-arms of the groom. There were plenty of unoccupied seats on the left hand side, however, with only Lucy, Colonel Aston's daughter, sitting on the front row and several of Adeline's servants seated towards the rear.

Everyone present was aware of Richard's occupation and many also knew of his personal closeness to the King, but that didn't prevent them all from being taken by surprise when the Royal Coach pulled up outside the church gates. The King had received an invitation, but it had been given as a matter of courtesy. Even Richard doubted that he would actually attend.

As the King entered into the church everyone immediately rose to their feet, just as if the bride herself had made her entrance. The two unnerved ushers, their bodies bent almost double, walked slowly backwards down the central aisle, leading the way to the front of the church. Those seated on the front row on the right hand side hurriedly made way and the chief usher gestured for the King to take a seat.

The King, however, had other ideas and chose to sit alongside Lucy on the left hand side.

The chief usher, a stickler for convention, attempted to remind the King of correct wedding etiquette. "The groom's guests are seated on the right, Your Majesty."

The King responded with a look of disdainful contempt and shooed the man away. "I am the King. I sit where I please," he said.

Suitably admonished, the chief usher bowed even lower and withdrew.

Just moments later the bride made her entrance. There were no bridesmaids or page boys. Adeline's sole escort was Colonel Aston who she had asked to stand in place of her father. The Colonel was fully aware of the truth of the situation of course, and therefore felt it necessary to consult the King on how he should respond to Adeline's request. The King was wholly supportive of the idea and said he could think of nobody he would rather have taking his place on such an occasion.

As tradition dictated, the bride was dressed all in white and walked down the aisle with her face covered by a thin veil. When she came alongside her groom he raised the veil and, almost immediately, Lucy found it necessary to offer the King her kerchief.

Wednesday 4th February 1685

The King's health had been failing for several days and there was growing concern about his well being. Richard was not surprised when he received a summons to urgently attend at his bedside. He arrived to find half a dozen physicians inflicting such manner of torture and indignities on the King that under any other circumstances he would have had them all immediately shot or put to the sword. The only other person present was Monsieur Allard, who appeared to be equally apalled and despairing of the situation

When the clearly ailing King observed that Richard had arrived, he instructed Allard to temporarily dismiss the physicians and beckoned Richard to draw close, so he could whisper in his ear. "I have decided that the time has come for Adeline to be informed of her true identity," he said, "and that it must be from my own lips that she hears it. I doubt she would believe it if she heard it from any others. Perhaps not even yours, Richard. Will you bring her to me?"

"Of course, Your Majesty, if that is your wish," Richard replied.

As Richard went to leave, Monsieur Allard grabbed his arm. "What will you tell Adeline in advance?" he asked.

Richard gave a faint shrug. "That, I do not know. I am bringing her to hear the well kept secrets of a dying man. How do I make that sound appealing?"

A short while later Richard returned, accompanied by Adeline and also their two year old son. Without prompting, Monsieur Allard again ushered the physicians out of the King's bedchamber before departing himself, leaving Richard and his family alone with the dying King.

Since her marriage to Richard, Adeline had met the King a number of times including, on occasion, in his private apartment, but she had never before entered into his bedchamber. She immediately noticed that her portrait, painted by Sir Godfrey Kneller, was hanging on the wall and she reacted with surprise. Although close to death, the King was still in full possession of his mental faculties and knew at once what she must be thinking. "It is an excellent likeness, is it not, Adeline?" he said. "And it also reminds me so much of your dear mother."

Adeline's surprise was now compounded. "You were acquainted with my mother, Your Majesty?"

The King had had many years to prepare himself for this occasion but, when it arrived, his words were entirely unrehearsed. "It was far more than mere acquaintanceship, Adeline," he said. "Your mother was my wife. And you are the product of our marriage."

For a moment Adeline was left speechless. When she recovered, the first words she spoke were addressed to Richard. "Did you know this?"

Richard said nothing, but merely nodded.

Adeline's confusion became suffused with anger. "Then why did you not tell me before?" she demanded.

"Do not be vexed with your husband, Adeline," said the King. "He was bound by oath not to reveal anything of what I have just told you. But he is now released from that oath and is free to tell you everything. What he does not know can be revealed by Monsieur Allard and Colonel Aston. And please do not judge me too harshly, either. Everything I have done, or not done, has been the result of a decision made from love. Always out of love for you and, more recently, also out of love for him." The King pointed at Richard and Adeline's son. "When you chose to name him Charles and asked me to be his Godfather, you have no idea how happy that made me. I was sorely tempted to tell you the truth on that occasion, but I knew the time was not right. Perhaps the time is still not right, but it grows ever shorter and I thought it important for you to hear it from my own lips. I doubt I shall have another opportunity. But now you must leave. My physicians, unwilling to let me die in peace, will be eager to return to my relentless torment. And I have no wish that you should be a witness to it."

Adeline, still struggling to come to terms with what she had just been told, leaned forward and kissed the King on the cheek, before lifting her son onto the bed to do the same.

As Adeline and her son left the bedchamber, the King beckoned Richard to draw close and whispered in his ear. "Take good care of them, Richard, and also of their secret. If Adeline's true identity becomes known, or even suspected, there will be few who wish her well, but many who wish her ill, including, no-doubt, even my own dear brother, James. From the day of my death you must not continue in military service. Immediately resign your commission and leave London as soon as possible. You and your family will be well provided for. In addition to a generous pension and gratuity that I have awarded to you, I have secretly bequeathed Adeline a substantial inheritance. Monsieur Allard and Colonel Aston are my joint executors and only they have knowledge of the details. Always remember that they are the only people who you should ever confide in, or consult, on any matter to do with Adeline. And finally, upon my death remove the portrait of Adeline and take it with you. It must not become the property of any other man."

Richard assured the King that he would comply fully with his wishes and protect Adeline and their son with his life.

Two days later, the King was dead.

THE PRESENT DAY

Day Seven - Sunday

It was shortly after noon and Archie Plum, creature of habit that he was, was where he could always be found at this time on any Sunday. He was sitting alone at a corner table in the Green Man Tavern, reading the post-mortem on yesterday's Crystal Palace match as he waited for the voluptuous Gloria to serve him his Sunday Dinner. Being no kind of cook himself, and having no spouse at home to cook for him, most weeks it was the only home cooked meal that he got to eat.

Archie had been married, twice in fact, but both wives had eventually thrown in the towel and taken the decision to divorce him. And not without good cause. From his early childhood until well into middle age Archie had been a thief. As he went in and out of jail, he had to learn the hard way that there was only so much of his absence that either one of his wives was prepared to tolerate.

But things were now very different. Archie was a reformed character treading a path as straight as one of Robin Hood's arrows, as he so often put it himself. And there was one person in particular he had to thank for helping him get onto that virtuous path and see the potential benefits of leading a more law-abiding life. That person was Ivor Jenkins, who, as a rookie constable, more than ten years earlier, had arrested Archie for the last time.

Jenkins had grown to be rather more cynical in recent years, but in the very earliest days of his police career he held the view that at least some of the people he arrested could transform their lives for the better. And he had been prepared to put some effort into helping them do that. Archie Plum had been the first man fortunate enough to receive the special Jenkins treatment and, as it turned out, he was also the last.

Following his final arrest and conviction Archie was sentenced to two years in prison, but, given his exemplary behaviour during his incarceration and some good words said on his behalf by Jenkins, he was allowed out on probation after only eight months. Whilst he was locked up, Jenkins visited him on a number of occasions and managed to convince him there was an alternative route for his life to take.

Whilst Jenkins could certainly claim much of the credit for persuading Archie to move off his road to perdition, his task was greatly eased by the fact that Archie excelled in one particular skill. Until his last period of imprisonment it was a skill that Archie had only ever used for illegal purposes, but Jenkins helped him see its potential for forming the basis of a legal and, quite possibly, highly lucrative career.

Soon after Archie was released on probation, Jenkins introduced him to an entertainment agent in the West End, one who specialised in providing acts for nightclub cabarets, cruise ship variety shows and corporate parties. Archie demonstrated his particular skill and the instantly impressed agent immediately signed him up, quite certain he could arrange work that would make money for both of them. Archie was delighted, but, knowing the agent had been informed of his criminal past, was surprised that he was prepared to take him onto his books quite so quickly. What Archie didn't know, was that the agent had himself done time, many years before, but had been given a second chance and was prepared to do the same for someone else, provided that both the person and the circumstances were right. In the case of Archie, he judged that they were.

More than a decade on, Archie was now well established in his legitimate, showbiz career. It had not made him rich, but it had managed to provide him with a degree of stability, comfort and security that he had never previously known. As his career developed, so had his ego and feelings of self-worth, to the extent that, in his own mind at least, he was now an 'arteeeeest'. And he attempted to present himself accordingly. His haitches were no longer dropped, 'fings' were replaced by 'things', and he pronounced the 'g', as required, at the end of all participles. And he had a dream of one day being properly discovered, with the prospect of hitting the big-time, perhaps performing to sell-out crowds in Las Vegas, doing Christmas specials on the TV, or scoring a hit at the Royal Variety Performance and being rewarded with a knighthood.

In so very many ways, Archie was a completely different man to the one that Jenkins had arrested all those years before. But there were a few things that hadn't changed: his support for Crystal Palace and his fondness for Sunday Dinner at the Green Man being two of them.

Jenkins and Coyte-Sherman entered the Green Man Tavern just as Gloria was delivering Archie's roast chicken dinner with all the trimmings.

Archie reacted with surprise. "Good heavens, Mr. Jenkins, you were the last person I was expecting to see here today. It has been a long time."

Jenkins introduced Coyte-Sherman as his associate, Mr. Brown, before telling Archie that he had come to ask for a favour. First though, he wanted Archie to give a demonstration of his special talent for the benefit of Mr. Brown. "I haven't told him yet what it is that you do," he said.

Archie put down his knife and fork and stepped away from the table slightly. He then gestured for Coyte-Sherman to move closer, placed his hands on his shoulders to manoeuvre him into the preferred position and handed him a pack of playing cards. "Give them a good shuffle, if you will Mr. White, then pick one at random and take a good look at it.......without letting me see it of course. Then put it in your right hand jacket pocket and put the rest of the pack in the left one."

Coyte-Sherman did as instructed. He then stood in silence with his arms folded.

Archie took a step forward and tapped lightly on each of Coyte-Sherman's jacket pockets. "Jack of Diamonds," he announced with a smile, before instantly returning to devouring his Sunday dinner.

"No it isn't," said a visibly unimpressed Coyte-Sherman. "It's the King of Spades."

Archie gave a faint shrug. "Oh well, you win some, you lose some, Mr. Green."

"Stop playing games, Archie," Jenkins demanded. "Give him back his stuff."

Archie put down his knife and fork for a second time before also placing Coyte-Sherman's wallet, keys and phone on the table.

"That's Archie's real talent," said Jenkins. "He's the world's best pickpocket, although these days, I'm glad to say, he only does it to entertain."

"And don't forget the card tricks, Mr. Jenkins," Archie insisted. "I'm pretty good at those as well."

"Well the pick-pocketing was impressive," said Coyte-Sherman, "I never suspected a thing. But now I know about it, you won't manage it a second time. Your attempt at a card trick, though, was decidedly unimpressive."

Archie grinned broadly. "You sure about that, Mr. Grey?"

Coyte-Sherman felt inside his jacket pockets. The left hand pocket was empty and inside his right hand pocket was the Jack of Diamonds.

"Looking for these?" asked Archie, placing the pack of cards on the table, with the King of Spades face-up on top.

"I told you he was good," said Jenkins.

Archie smiled. "So, what's this favour you want, Mr. Jenkins?"

Jenkins handed him a photograph of Vincent Cotham. "We want you to pick the pockets of this man. To be precise, we want his phone."

Again Archie smiled. "Picking pockets is illegal, Mr. Jenkins. You can go to jail for that, you know."

"We don't want you to steal anything, Archie," said Jenkins. "We just want you to borrow his phone, for at most eight minutes. Then you can return it. What do you say?"

"Where and when do you want it done?" Archie asked.

"Tomorrow morning. Just after eight o'clock. On the Victoria Line, between Warren Street and Vauxhall," Jenkins replied.

Archie continued eating his dinner, considering the request, before eventually responding. "Suppose I agree to do it, what's the risk to me? Who is he? He's not some hard case gangster is he? I've grown quite attached to my genitals over the years."

"I think your genitals are quite safe," said Jenkins. "He's a sort of civil servant, but I don't think you need to know any more than that. In any case, you're the very best Archie, so he'll never know. That's why we're asking you to do it."

Archie eventually agreed. "Okay, Mr. Jenkins. I wouldn't do it for anybody else, but I'll do it for you."

"Excellent," said Coyte-Sherman. "Let me get you another drink."

"Thanks. I'll have a large scotch," responded Archie. "Oh, and if you're going to the bar, Mr. Black, you'll need this." Archie handed Coyte-Sherman his wallet, before placing the Major's phone and keys on the table for the second time.

Brazelle's Sunday morning sermon was far from being one of his best. He had got very little sleep the night before as he repeatedly went over in his mind the incredible story he had read in Sir Bernard's Journal, endlessly mulling over its implications. After the morning service he returned home to put the finishing touches to his planned evening sermon, hoping he could make a better job of it. He'd barely started on it when the phone rang.

Frances was on the line, sounding quite excited. "After discovering a painting by a famous portrait artist who had connections to the Royal Court, I began to wonder what it might be worth. So I got in touch with an old friend of my father who used to be an art dealer. Although he retired years ago he still has lots of contacts and he very kindly put me in touch with a chap called John Simms. He's a professor of Fine Art and reckoned to be an expert on the work of Sir Godfrey Kneller. When I told him I'd come across a Kneller portrait, believed to be my eleven times great grandmother, Lady Adeline Harfield, he seemed very interested. He said it was one he'd never heard of. I've invited him to come over tomorrow morning to take a look at it. I have to say, though, I was a bit disappointed when he told me that most Kneller's only sell for between ten and twenty thousand. Although he did say that the more unusual ones can go for a bit more, especially if there's a good story to tell about them."

"If he's an expert, then at least he should be able to confirm that it really is one of Kneller's," said Brazelle. "Not that I think it might be a fake. And I reckon this one does have a pretty good back story. I'll be interested to hear what he has to say about it."

Brazelle took the opportunity of letting Frances know that he had discovered Sir Bernard's journals and had started to read them. However he managed to buy himself more time by promising to do some further reading and then give a report of his findings to both Harfield sisters after Rose returned from the US. He hoped he wasn't making himself a hostage to fortune, but thought he had little choice other than to make such a commitment.

The journals were the property of the Harfield sisters and Brazelle knew he would have to hand them over at some point. They were far from an easy read, but he thought it still highly likely that, sooner or later, one or other of the sisters would get round to reading through them. It therefore seemed pointless to consider leaving out any of the details when he came to give his report, regardless of how incredible some of those details appeared to be. The real challenge he faced was deciding how to present his report, not what to leave out of it. To help him come to a conclusion on the way forward he felt he needed to do some more research and then seek advice from someone he could trust and whose judgement he respected. He had just the right person in mind.

Later that day, feeling he had done a much better job delivering his evening sermon than he had done in the morning, Brazelle returned home to take his first look at his Sunday paper and read a lengthy article reporting on Julie's murder. It had previously been made public that Julie had been strangled, but the newspaper article added one further detail – she had been strangled with one of her own scarves. The police had confirmed there were no signs of a break-in, or evidence to suggest the murderer had a sexual or robbery motive. And apart from the body of the murdered victim, the only other signs of violence were the shattered remains of a glass vase that had been smashed against a wall, leaving its contents strewn around the room, and pieces of two ripped photographs that were also scattered about. There was also one further revelation. Police had discovered that Julie had been living in Eastbourne using a false identity.

Day Eight - Monday

Coyte-Sherman, Jenkins and Archie all arrived at Warren Street well before eight and when Cotham arrived they followed him into the same tube carriage.

Unfortunately, the train was even more crowded than usual and it took Archie rather longer than expected to get himself in the right position to do his job. By the time he handed Cotham's phone to Coyte-Sherman almost two minutes had passed.

"He's an odd kind of civil servant, Mr. Jenkins," whispered Archie. "He's wearing a shoulder holster and carrying a semi-automatic with a silencer. My genitals are becoming decidedly twitchy."

Jenkins was genuinely surprised. "I swear we weren't expecting that, Archie."

Archie gave a shrug. "Well, it's too late to change my mind now. What's done is done. What exactly have you got to do?"

Coyte-Sherman quickly connected Cotham's phone to a device in his pocket. "We download what's on his phone using this gizmo and slip in a trojan."

"Suppose his phone rings?" said Archie.

"Whilst it's wired up to this, it won't," replied Coyte-Sherman. "If anybody calls, they'll just get a no service signal."

Having discovered that Cotham was armed, the normally relaxed Archie was getting ever more edgy. "And what if he decides he wants to make a call himself?" he asked.

"Then we'll need to change his mind," said Coyte-Sherman. "You two keep an eye on him. If he starts rummaging through his pockets, like he's looking for something, create some sort of distraction. That's something you're supposed to be good at, isn't it Archie? I'll be done in three minutes."

The train was just leaving Pimlico and Jenkins was also becoming edgy. "We haven't got three minutes," he said.

Two minutes later, the train pulled into Vauxhall. With barely a second to spare, Coyte-Sherman handed the phone to Archie who immediately hurried towards the open carriage doors. He arrived just in time to step onto the platform alongside Cotham, brushing against him as he did. Cotham walked away, apparently unaware of what had just happened. And Archie gave the thumbs-up sign to his two partners in crime, just as their train pulled out of the station.

Jenkins and Coyte-Sherman were relieved. The operation appeared to have been a success and they could hardly believe their luck. They now had a mass of potentially useful data to work through and the ability to monitor Cotham's every move. On the other hand their successful enterprise had uncovered a new matter of concern and Jenkins was the first to raise it. "Cotham is obviously not just a pen-pushing middle ranking diplomat at the US Embassy. Not if he takes a gun with a silencer to the office."

Coyte-Sherman agreed. "The gun I could just about understand. Being an American diplomat, even a fairly minor one, isn't the safest job in the world these days, so the gun could be for personal protection. But there's certainly no need for a silencer."

"He's CIA. Isn't he?" Jenkins suggested.

"Or something even worse," said Coyte-Sherman.

Professor Simms arrived at Harfield House at exactly eleven o'clock. Frances thought his punctuality commendable, but she was somewhat taken aback by his physical appearance. On his feet he had a pair of bright orange shoes and he was wearing a rather garish apricot suit, paired with a heavily flowered mustard cravat. And he had a pink silk handkerchief dangling from his top left-hand jacket pocket. The hairstyle he was sporting was equally unexpected. It was a rather magnificent Mohican. None of it was at all what Frances was expecting for the look of a celebrated Professor of Fine Art. Had her late father's art dealer friend not personally recommended the man, she would almost certainly have had her doubts about the wisdom of inviting him into her home. As it was, she had her reservations anyway.

Simms took almost twenty minutes examining the portrait of Lady Adeline, before eventually giving his judgement. "My first impression is that it is a genuine Kneller," he said. "However, if I am to confirm my opinion beyond the bounds of dubiety, I shall need to take it away and do some minor tests. They're quite unobtrusive. It will be X-rayed and the paint will undergo chemical analysis, using the merest macula of the medium. I shall assign it as a project for one of my postgraduate students to undertake. But rest assured, madam, I shall be at all times in charge of proceedings."

"And, if it is genuine, what might it be worth?" asked Frances.

"A much harder question to answer," Simms replied. "As I mentioned on the telephone, these days most Knellers go for between ten and twenty thousand pounds. However, this one could turn out to have a value that is considerably greater. It possesses a plenitude of unique features. The inclusion of the portrait of King Charles in the background, for example, can only be described as sui generis, with regard to the work of Kneller. The full meaning and significance of its presence is really quite difficult to comprehend, but must surely indicate some close association between the portrait's subject and the King. It is a facsimile of a portrait of Charles that Kneller painted very shortly after his return to the throne. If my initial assessment is correct and the portrait is a genuine Kneller, then the King himself must have demanded that his portrait be included. Kneller himself would never have dared even ask for it to be incorporated and the idea he would have inserted it without the King's permission is too preposterous to consider, especially when it appears alongside symbols of Catholicism. The same can also be said of the jewellery that the woman is wearing. The last time I saw those rubies, they were adorning an image of Charles' mother, Queen Henrietta Maria, in another of Kneller's portraits."

Once Professor Simms had departed with Adeline's portrait and Frances had recovered from the shock of meeting him she phoned Brazelle. After telling him about her meeting with the eccentric Simms she had one further piece of news to impart.

"I've managed to get some information on the coat of arms that appears on the two chest lids we found," she said. "It isn't as much as we might have hoped for, but it's better than nothing. Apparently the black lion with red claws that appears in one quadrant is what's called a Flemish Lion and its presence almost certainly indicates an association with north eastern France. My informant, an associate of

Damien, has been extremely helpful and done quite a lot of research to try and track it down further, but has been unsuccessful. He thinks it most likely that it was the Coat of Arms of some family of minor French gentry who once lived not very far from the Belgian border, but who have long since died out. He says that a lot of the documentation that might have helped to identify the family concerned may have been destroyed during, or just after, the French Revolution. But who knows?"

Sunday night had been yet another extremely restless one for Brazelle. He'd spent sleepless hours deliberating on the implications of what he'd read in the first of Sir Bernard's journals, whilst also considering what he should do with the letter he'd discovered hidden with them. And that wasn't all. After reading the Sunday newspaper report on Julie's murder he had begun to completely reconsider his thoughts on that matter. With his brain in semi-overdrive it had been impossible for him to sleep, but by the time dawn arrived he thought his hours spent awake hadn't been entirely wasted. By late morning, after copious consumption of coffee, several phone calls and much time spent on his computer he had decided on a plan of action. He was just about to get started working his way through it when the phone rang. Frances was keen to tell him about her visit from Professor Simms that had just ended.

Everything that Professor Simms had told Frances appeared to Brazelle to fit well with what he had read in Sir Bernard's Journal. He was particularly intrigued by what Simms had said about the jewellery Adeline was wearing in the portrait. Whatever happened to that?

"Are you quite sure you've never had sight of those rubies anywhere other than in the portraits of Adeline and Justine?" Brazelle asked. "Not even a fleeting glance?"

"I'm quite certain that I haven't," Frances replied. "And I have absolutely no doubt that I would remember if I had. They're really quite magnificent. If they really did once belong to my ancestors and got passed down to my father then he kept very quiet about it and kept them very well hidden. And, for goodness sake Chris, why would he do that?"

Frances had just asked a very good question. But there was an even better one - where were the rubies now?

Brazelle was grateful to receive Frances's report of her meeting with her chosen expert, but decided not tell her that he was about to consult an expert of his own.

Professor Graham Davey of Oxford University is generally acknowledged to be one of the world's foremost experts on the life and times of King Charles the Second. Having spent almost three decades researching every aspect of the King's existence, he had managed to gather together enough material to author numerous academic papers and publish three books on his specialist subject. His volumes: King Charles in Exile; King Charles in Battle; and, King Charles in the Bedchamber; had all been very well received. The third in particular was a major best-seller.

Professor Davey was in his study listening to the radio when Brazelle arrived for his planned meeting. The news bulletin had just ended and there was a return to the Test Match cricket commentary.

"Are you a cricket fan, Mr. Brazelle?" asked the professor.

Brazelle shook his head. "No. I can't say that I am."

Davey turned off the radio. "Neither am I, especially when it's on the wireless. It comes second only to the Shipping Forecast on the boredom scale, in my humble opinion."

Brazelle doubted that Professor Davey had ever had an opinion that could have been described as humble.

"Anyway, you haven't come to discuss cricket, have you, Mr. Brazelle? When we spoke on the phone you said you had some questions about Charles the Second you wished to ask me."

Brazelle got straight to the point. "I was wondering if you'd ever come across any evidence, however scant, that Charles the Second got married during the period of his forced exile in France."

Professor Davey leaned back in his chair. "When you asked if you could pay me a visit to ask a few questions about Charles the Second, I did consider one or two things you might want to enquire about, but I didn't contemplate that one. However, since you ask, the answer is an emphatic, no. But why do you ask? Have you turned up some evidence yourself?"

"Perhaps," Brazelle replied. "Whilst researching the family history of some friends of mine, I came across an old family journal. There's an entry stating that King Charles secretly married a Catholic woman in the French village of Bollezeele in March 1659. The journal also claims that Charles's wife died a few days after giving birth to a daughter in December of that year, although the child survived."

Fascinating indeed," said Davey. "And the family whose history you were researching when you came across this journal, would it happen to be the Harfield family?"

Brazelle was taken by surprise. "What makes you think it might be?" he asked.

Professor Davey smiled. "That sounds very much like a 'yes' to me," he said. "But let me explain. When we spoke on the phone you mentioned that you lived in Prinsted. It was for that reason I was so quick to agree to meet with you. Whilst I was studying for my doctorate, almost thirty years ago, I visited Prinsted to interview Sir Cornelius Harfield. At the time, my research was focussed on Charles the Second's last few years of life. It was the period when

Sir Richard Harfield, Sir Cornelius's ancestor, was commander of the King's bodyguard. In such a role Sir Richard was likely to have known just about all of Charles's secrets. I was hoping that some of those secrets might have been passed down through the Harfield generations, eventually reaching Sir Cornelius, and that he might be willing to share them with me. Sadly it was not to be. Sir Cornelius was courteous and polite throughout our meeting, but extremely tight-lipped about all aspects of his family history. I left Prinsted with very little to show for my efforts, apart from two very clear impressions. First, that Sir Cornelius knew far more about the life and times of Sir Richard than he admitted. And second, that he'd only agreed to meet with me so he could find out how much I already knew about his illustrious ancestor. When you mentioned both Prinsted and King Charles in the same brief phone-call I instantly recalled the connection. A bit of a coincidence, don't you think? It made me wonder if the current Harfield generation would be more forthcoming than Sir Cornelius ever was, and that I might be able to add one more chapter to my doctoral thesis. Actually, if what you've just told me is verifiably true, I will need to write a lot more than just one extra chapter. But what about this journal you've found? Who wrote it? Can I see it for myself?"

"My reason for coming here today was only to get your opinion as to whether or not there was the remotest possibility that the story could be true," said Brazelle. "I hadn't intended to mention the Harfield family. But you've guessed right. The journal does belong to them. It was written by the Fourth Baronet Harfield. He claimed the entry I referred to was dictated to him by his great-grandmother Adeline, widow of Sir Richard. If I do show it to you it must be with the family's consent, but at the moment they know absolutely nothing of the journal's claims and I haven't told anyone that I've consulted you."

Given the circumstances, Brazelle decided he might as well also tell Davy about Lady Adeline's portrait and what Professor Simms had had to say about it, especially in relation to the jewellery Adeline was wearing.

"I'm acquainted with Simms," said Davy. "I've met him a couple of times. As I recall, he's a rather eccentric dresser who possesses a particularly brutal handshake. But be that as it may, he does know his stuff when it comes to Kneller and I'm sure he'd recognise Queen Henrietta Maria's wedding jewellery if he saw it. According to the historical record, the Queen gave it to Charles during his exile in France. And nothing has been heard of it since. It's always been assumed that Charles sold it, perhaps having first broken it up so it couldn't be identified, and then used the proceeds to pay his bills. What you've just told me rather puts a question mark over that assumption. On the other hand, just because Kneller included it in one of his portraits in 1681 doesn't prove it still existed at that time. He had previously painted it adorning Queen Henrietta Maria herself and was therefore well acquainted with it. Painters in all generations have occasionally been guilty of making an artistic tweak."

Davey took down an atlas from his bookshelf and opened it at a page showing a map of north east France. "Bollezeele is barely twenty kilometres from St Omer," he said. "Together with everything else you've told me, especially the dates you mentioned, that does make the story marginally more plausible." He went on to explain. "Over the years, the life of Charles the Second has been the subject of so much research that one has to wonder if there's very much left to learn about the man. However, there is one brief period in his life that remains shrouded in mystery. Although, for reasons of security, Charles never stayed very long at any one location, his time in exile has been fairly well documented. Right up until the day he suddenly disappeared, that is. One day in late 1658 he was in Paris, with his presence there witnessed by at least a dozen people, but the next day he'd vanished. It wasn't until around six months later that he resurfaced. When he did, it was in St Omer, about twelve months before his return to England to reclaim his throne. And there's no evidence, of which I'm aware, that he ever revealed his whereabouts or told anyone what he'd been doing during the time he was missing. Even his closest friends and confidants claimed ignorance, although it's hard to believe that the commander of his bodyguard at the time, Colonel Aston, and his private secretary, Allard, didn't know where he was. I'm sure you can see how all this fits in very snugly with the story you've just told me, Mr. Brazelle. That doesn't prove anything, of course, but it does suggest it might be worth probing a little more deeply. If it is true and we can prove it, well, it could be the historian's equivalent of the opening of Tutankhamun's tomb."

"Before I arrived here, I was fairly convinced you would quickly tear the story to shreds," said Brazelle, "but you've just done the exact opposite. Do you have any suggestions for the next step to take in order to probe more deeply, as you put it?"

"Yes, I most certainly do," Davy replied. "Unlike you, I'm not a religious man, Mr. Brazelle, but that does not preclude me from knowing a thing or two about the workings of the

Catholic Church. It may very well be an institution with a number of shortcomings, but its bureaucratic expertise has always been second to none. If Charles was married in a French Catholic Church, I have little doubt that a written record of the event would have been made at the time and Charles Stuart would have been required to put his signature to it. The christening of a daughter and the death and burial of her mother would also have been documented. Documents, Mr. Brazelle, can be as manna from Heaven for any historian. If those events did take place and the confirming documents still exist, then we must find them. Obviously, after almost four hundred years, such a quest will indeed be a challenge. The person chosen to lead it must possess qualities of perspicacity, perseverance and single-mindedness. And they must also be fluent in French. Fortunately, I know just the right person for the job."

"And who is that?" asked Brazelle.

"Me!" Professor Davey replied.

The meeting with Professor Davey had not concluded the way Brazelle expected that it would, but it had certainly been worthwhile. After promising to give the Professor sight of Sir Bernard's journal just as soon as he had got permission from its owners, the Harfield family, he prepared to leave.

"Just before you go, Mr. Brazelle, I'm intrigued to know why you chose to consult me in particular on this matter," said Davey.

"I went online and searched for experts on the life of King Charles. Your name came up second."

"Only second!" Davey exclaimed. "And whose name, pray tell me, came ahead of mine?"

"Professor Nicholas Penhaligon. But I couldn't consult him because he died six months ago. Did you know him?"

"Sadly, yes," Davey replied. "He was a peevish little man with a misplaced sense of adequacy. For some years we were on opposite sides of an academic debate over the true causes of the English Civil War."

"And which side of the debate were you on?" asked Brazelle.

"The correct one," Professor Davey replied.

Major Daniel Coyte-Sherman heads a small highly secretive team within Military Intelligence and reports directly to the Head of that service. Although he has a great deal of autonomy in how he runs his unit it is not without limit, one that lately he had most definitely exceeded. Over the past week he and his team had become heavily involved in an unauthorised operation and were also harbouring two fugitives. It was only a matter of time before his CO started asking questions. His only chance of justifying his actions and surviving with his career intact was to quickly produce some worthwhile results. Uncovering a spy at the American Embassy was a good start, but if he could identify Austin, the traitor in the senior ranks of the Metropolitan Police Service, then that would certainly do the trick.

With the trojan successfully installed on Cotham's phone, his movements could be tracked, his calls monitored and his messages intercepted. From now on he would have no privacy. And since the data downloaded from his phone included his personal schedule and address book, together with his call log and all those messages he had chosen to save, much of his recent past was also open to scrutiny. Coyte-Sherman and Jenkins worked their way through it all, looking for any nugget of information that might help in their quest to identify Austin.

In his trawl through the phone's call log, one phone number in particular had caught Jenkins' interest. Although it wasn't listed in the phone's address book, there had been several calls either made to it, or received from it, during the hours immediately prior to the raid on the safe-house. And there had been one very brief call made to it in the early hours of the morning following the attack.

The number was investigated by Sergeant Kim Robinson, one of Coyte-Sherman's technical staff. She quickly discovered it belonged to an unregistered pay-as-you-go phone, so she was unable to connect it to any named owner. However, she was able to identify the phone's current whereabouts. "It's somewhere in or around number 8, Broadway, Westminster. Postcode SW1H 0BG," she reported.

"And what sort of building is that?" asked Coyte-Sherman.

"A bloody great big one," said Jenkins with a smile. "It's New Scotland Yard."

The trojan in Cotham's phone gave Sergeant Robinson total control over all of its functions. Not only could she monitor all calls and messages coming in to, or going out of the phone, but she could also block them if she chose to, and Cotham would be none the wiser. She could also send messages or make calls that would register on the recipient's phone as having come from Cotham's phone. It was a scammer's dream.

Gant had given his interrogators details of the few brief face-to-face meetings he had had with Cotham, who he only knew by the codename Seattle. He confirmed that all meetings had taken place late at night in Regent's Park and at short notice, following his receipt of a text message. Seattle invariably demanded a reply confirming that his summons had been received and would be complied with, and always signed off with a single capital letter S.

There was no guarantee that Cotham managed his relationship with Austin in exactly the same way that he dealt with Gant, but it was all that Coyte-Sherman had to work with and time was running short. He wrote a summons of his own and handed it to Sergeant Robinson. "Send this to the phone at New Scotland Yard and make sure it's Cotham's phone number that's identified as the sender. Then block all contact between the two phones. I don't want any chance that my cunning plan gets cocked-up because they have some genuine communication."

The message Robinson sent read: 'Essential you meet me 9pm tonight at The Ready Money Drinking Fountain in Regent's Park. Reply to confirm. S'

Almost sixty anxious minutes later, the much hoped for reply arrived: 'Message received. A'

Jenkins knew he could not play a central role in the planned sting operation. He would have to leave the handling of the main event to Coyte-Sherman and Sergeant Robinson whilst he remained in radio communication with the pair, out of sight in a van parked on the other side of the nearby Gloucester Gate.

It was just coming up to nine o'clock as Coyte-Sherman and his female companion sat down on one of the park benches that gave them an uninterrupted view of the Ready Money Drinking Fountain. There were other people still about in the Park: joggers; dog walkers; and, the occasional skateboarder, but Coyte-Sherman and Sergeant Robinson were the only ones not actually moving. In their attempt to look unexceptional and not draw any attention to themselves they casually chatted about nothing in particular, whilst keeping a close eye on what was happening around the Fountain and whispering the occasional update to Jenkins.

The minutes went by, but nobody approached the Fountain. By five minutes past nine, Coyte-Sherman was becoming anxious. Was it to be a no-show? Had Austin smelled a rat? He and Robinson were both pretty much novices at this surveillance business, being essentially back-office operators, so was it possible they'd given themselves away somehow? Coyte-Sherman began to think how he himself might behave if he were summoned to an assignation in the Park. Would he go straight to the designated spot and hang about there until the other person turned up? Or would he wait at a place nearby, where he could watch for their arrival? He decided that the latter was as likely as the former and looked around for any likely candidates. That's when he noticed, for the first time, a lone figure sitting on a bench, some distance away, on the other side of the Fountain. It seemed an odd thing to do, to sit alone in the semi darkness in an almost empty park, not long before closing time. Odd that is, unless they were there to meet someone. It was impossible to immediately tell very much about the individual as they were over fifty yards away and in a particularly dark spot. Coyte-Sherman marked them as a definite person of interest, but decided to wait a few more minutes before going to take a closer look at them, just in case someone else showed up. In the event, the only other people who did appear were two park keepers, preparing to lock up the park gates for the night.

"We'll be told to leave the park in a couple of minutes," Coyte-Sherman told Sergeant Robinson. "Let's take a closer look at the person sitting over there before that happens. I can't see any other possible suspects."

Just as Coyte-Sherman and Robinson prepared to move, their person of interest stood up and headed at speed towards the Gloucester Gate. At the pace they were going they would be out through the gates and gone in seconds. Coyte-Sherman hastily radioed Jenkins who responded immediately. He jumped out of the van and rushed towards the Gloucester Gate from the other direction, arriving just in time to make an interception. Shocked to see who it was, he was momentarily left speechless, but quickly recovered.

"Good evening, Mrs. McAllister," he said. "What on earth brings you here?"

Day Nine - Tuesday

Brazelle had experienced a much more settled and restful night. He was still fast asleep when he was woken by the ringing of his phone.

"I have some good news," said Jenkins. "Last night we identified and arrested Austin."

Before Jenkins could say anymore, Brazelle, now fully awake, interrupted. "Let me guess...........Mrs. McAllister?"

Jenkins was surprised. "How did you know?"

"Well, I can't say that I actually knew for sure," said Brazelle, "but, given her privileged position, she certainly had to be included on any shortlist of suspects. And she'd definitely worked her way to the top of mine. For the reasons I gave before, I couldn't put my faith in your theory that the traitor was either Harris or Brompton. If it had been one of them, I'm convinced the raid on the safe-house would have happened much sooner. As far as I was concerned, the traitor had to be either someone who had only very recently found out where Gant was being held, or someone who knew that the Commissioner was about to go there and somehow arranged for his journey to be tracked. Given that the raid took place within just a few minutes of your arrival at the safe-house, the second option seemed to me to be the most likely. And that immediately made Mrs.

McAllister a very strong candidate. The Commissioner's decision to make the trip was very last minute, so who else would know about it? You told me how secretive he was about the matter, so it seemed highly unlikely he'd tell anyone else where he was going, except perhaps for Harris and Brompton. Why would he need to? And you assured me that you didn't tell anyone. But, if it was Mrs. McAllister, one question remained: how did she arrange for the journey to be tracked? The answer, of course, is the pen. And her timing for giving it to the Commissioner was brilliant. He was in your car and on the point of leaving, so it was almost certain he'd be taking it with him. The pen's packaging and the card that came with it were chosen to increase the probability of that happening. McAllister may not have known Julie's identity, but she was Sir Andrew's PA and would, at the very least, have noticed clues suggesting he had a lover tucked away somewhere. But even if she was wrong about that, it was of no real concern. The pen would be in the car and that was all that mattered. Without him realising it, Sir Andrew was Cotham's source at the top of the Met. No doubt that's why Cotham referred to Austin using male pronouns. The sly, eavesdropping and treacherous Mrs. McAllister was just the means by which the information was gathered and communicated. It was Sir Andrew who was the real source. But tell me the rest, Ifor. What's happening about Vincent Cotham?"

"He should be landing in the States just about now," replied Jenkins. "The CIA certainly doesn't hang about. As soon as we were sure we had Austin, Daniel let his CIA contact know why we were interested in Cotham. That was around ten o'clock last night. By midnight they'd grabbed him and put him on a US Air Force plane direct to Virginia. It turns out he was one of their own, not just some ordinary middle-ranking member of the US diplomatic service. According to the CIA chap they intend to throw the book at him and charge him with treason. That's a Federal capital offence. He'll face the death penalty."

"No he won't," Brazelle objected. "He'll make a deal. They always do. He's not a soldier of conscience, fighting for some holy or political cause. He's a mercenary. You can tell that from the type of organisation he's involved with. They're into personal power and treasure and so will he be. Trust me, Ifor, whatever he knows so will the CIA by the end of the week."

"I defer to your greater experience of such matters," said Jenkins. "And if you're right, then the people at the top of the organisation should be identified. According to Gant, if you remember, Cotham claimed to have met with all three of them."

Brazelle agreed. "Yes, I remember. And identifying them should lead to the destruction of the whole organisation. But where does this leave you? And what about Gant and his wife?"

"Thankfully, I'm not the prime suspect in seven murders anymore. My story of what went on at the safe-house is finally being believed. I've been able to return to my office at the Yard and move back into my flat. I've even been able to put the battery back in my mobile phone and start communicating with the world again. As for Gant and his wife, she's been put in protective custody and he's being held on remand in a high security prison with a small army guarding him. DC Brompton hasn't taken the secrecy and seclusion approach that the Chief took. But once the key players in Cotham's organisation have been identified and neutralised the level of threat should be significantly reduced."

"And what about Danny?" Brazelle asked. "I assume he's now told his CO what he's been up to this past week?"

"I guess he must have done," replied Jenkins. "He said that at one point he'd got to thinking he might get court-martialled and cashiered, maybe even forfeiting his army pension. Now, though, he thinks he might be given a medal and get promoted to lieutenant-colonel!"

Later that day Brazelle learned that he had called it right. Cotham did make a deal to save his life. The only detail he got wrong was the speed with which the terms of his deal were agreed. It all happened much quicker than Brazelle had expected and Cotham was already providing all kinds of useful information about the organisation of which he, Ted Gant and Grace McAllister had all been members.

Although Coyte-Sherman's CIA contact was not authorised to disclose names, he was able to confirm that Cotham had divulged the identity of several members of the organisation including, most importantly, the three people at its head. Who says there is honour amongst thieves? And he had admitted to being the handler of Mrs. McAllister and passing on information that she had supplied. In fact, he pleaded guilty to just about everything that was put to him, but with one exception. He denied having anything to do with the murder of Julie, or even knowing of her existence.

Jenkins and Coyte-Sherman had assumed it was either Cotham, or someone acting on his orders, who had murdered Julie. Hearing of his denial they were forced to think again. If he was complicit, then why would he deny it? He had made his deal, so why not own up to his involvement in one more murder amongst many? Unless, of course, he really hadn't been involved.

The only person who was not surprised by Cotham's denial of involvement in Julie's murder was Brazelle. Just like Jenkins, when he first heard of Julie's murder, he thought it likely that her killer was in some way connected to the organisation of which Gant had been a member. What he later learned about Julie's background and the circumstances surrounding her death, however, forced him to think again.

He had now come up with an entirely different theory. One that Jenkins, a highly competent and experienced police officer, would probably also have arrived at, had he not been forced by circumstances to commit his time and energy to other, more pressing, matters over the past few days.

Brazelle was convinced he now knew the motive behind Julie's murder and the identity of her killer. After making just a few more enquiries he was confident that he would have the matter resolved.

Day Ten - Wednesday

Brazelle had stayed up late the night before, working on his portrait of Rose. He was still clinging to a faint hope that he might get it finished by the time she returned on Thursday evening, but that hope was fading fast. There were also a number of other loose ends he was keen to tie up before she returned. And of course he still had his duties as the acting parish priest to fulfill. He had been in far more pressured situations in the past, including some that had him placed in harm's way, but that didn't stop him wishing he had more time to get everything finished. Fortunately, he was about to get it.

Rose phoned from New York to say that her return to England would unfortunately have to be delayed, most probably until the following Monday. There had been a last minute hitch with the sale of her business. It was nothing she couldn't deal with, but getting matters completed was going to take a little longer than she had originally assumed. Sensing Brazelle's disappointment she promised to make it up to him when she returned.

Brazelle was actually left with mixed feelings. He had been very much looking forward to Rose's return the following evening but, on the other hand, he would now have more time to complete her portrait and also tie up those other loose ends.

Having heard that Lee Northcott, the Harfield Estate Manager, had returned earlier than expected from his

Himalayan vacation, Brazelle went over to the Estate Management Office on the High Street to pay him a visit. He was surprised to find Northcott sitting behind his desk with his left leg, encased in plaster-of-paris, resting on it.

"I was going to ask if you'd had a good holiday," said Brazelle, "but now I'm not sure how tactful a question that would be."

"Thank you for your concern, Reverend," Northcott responded. "I'm afraid that my lifelong yearning to be the first Englishman to reach the peak of Everest wearing a Chelsea strip has been thwarted by a slight disagreement with a rather large rock. Have you come on a pastoral visit to commiserate with me?"

"To be honest, no. I'd heard that you had returned earlier than expected from your vacation, but I didn't know about your broken leg until I just walked in, or, for that matter, your lifelong yearning. I came to ask if I could have the jeep back."

Northcott threw him the keys. "I don't see why not, especially since you're practically a member of the family these days. I was surprised when I found it parked round the back and those keys pushed through the letterbox."

Brazelle picked up the keys. "Thanks. And, since one good turn definitely deserves another, especially given your current situation, if there's anything I can do to help just let me know."

"Well, since you're offering, there's something you could do for me straightaway, Reverend." Northcott pushed a small pile of paper files across the desk and placed a large key on top. "These need to be put in the strong-room in the basement, but in my current condition it's a bit difficult for me to get down there. Don't worry where you put them. Anywhere in there will do."

Brazelle had visited the Harfield Estate Office on a number of occasions, but this was the first time he'd gone down into the basement. The greater part of the space was taken up by the strong-room and behind its thick steel door was row upon row of shelves, each stacked with folders, files and boxes, many clearly very old. Brazelle was particularly struck by the apparent absence of any systematic organisation. After returning upstairs he asked Northcott how he ever managed to find anything.

"I don't," said Northcott. "The place is like one of them black holes. Stuff goes in, but nothing ever comes out. Anything that's likely to be needed again gets kept by the family's lawyers. Everything else ends up in the strong-room downstairs. It's how it's always been. Call it custom and practice. Some of the stuff down there must go back centuries. Bills of sale, letters, invoices, old rental agreements, you name it and it'll be down there. Maybe one day somebody will get round to going through it all. But it won't be me."

"Presumably the strong-room was created when this place was a bank?" said Brazelle. "Do you know when that was?"

"The Harfield Bank was established on July 1st, 1803, to be precise," replied Northcott. "It was the brainchild of Sir William, the Fifth Baronet. There were lots of other banks being created about that time and he must have decided to get in on the act. You can tell by the sheer size of the strong-room he must have had big ideas about making lots of money. Unfortunately his ideas turned out to be delusions. Within five years his Bank had lost him pretty close to half his fortune. That's when he shot himself. He couldn't face the shame of it all, I suppose. Then his son Philip, the Sixth Baronet, closed the Bank and turned this place into the Harfield Estate Office. And that's what it's been ever since. I suppose some of the stuff in the strong-room must date to that far back at least."

After leaving the Harfield Estate Office Brazelle drove to Abingdon, to 17 Mansfield Avenue, to be precise. There was a black Mercedes parked on the drive. After knocking on the front door several times, but getting no response, he went around to the rear of the building where, fortunately, he discovered that the back door had been left unlocked.

The test match commentary was blaring out of the kitchen radio. "England needs one hundred and fifty runs to avoid an ignominious defeat, but have only two tail-end batsmen left to get them," screeched the clearly partisan cricket commentator.

Brazelle, although knowing very little about cricket, sensed England's imminent humiliation. But that wasn't all he could sense. After checking each of the downstairs rooms he went upstairs to where the stench was strongest. In what he took to be the master bedroom he found what he had come looking for and had expected to find. Lying on the bed was the body of a man in his mid-fifties. A drained whisky bottle and an empty bottle of pills were on the bedside cabinet together with a handwritten note. Brazelle read the note then phoned Chief Inspector Jenkins.

Another loose end to be tied up was the keeping of the promise Brazelle had made to Dr. Gerald Caulfield several days earlier. Later that day he called to see him to explain what had happened to Gant and, more importantly, reassure him that he no longer needed to fear being charged with giving aid and comfort to a fugitive from justice and be struck off the Medical Register.

Caulfield was understandably relieved and poured two large whiskies by way of celebration.

The easing of Gerald's stress wasn't the only reason for Brazelle's visit. It was also the ideal time for him to raise a couple of other sensitive matters. He began by showing Gerald Sir Bernard's journals and recounted the tale they told.

Gerald listened attentively until Brazelle had completed his narrative but was then quick to express his incredulity. "To say the story is hard to believe is an understatement. I find it much easier to believe that either the old lady was a mad fantasist or Sir Bernard was a total liar."

"Well, those are definitely a couple of possibilities," said Brazelle. "But, if the story is true, then it would explain where Sir Richard Harfield's great wealth came from. And there are a few other bits of circumstantial evidence that tend to give it some credibility."

Brazelle told Gerald about the painting, believed to be a portrait of Lady Adeline, and about the secret passageways he had discovered. And how he believed the passageway leading from the old basement into the nearby woods was originally created by Sir Richard Harfield, as a means of escape from anyone who discovered Adeline's true identity and came to do her harm.

"Hold on a minute, Chris. You might be making the wrong connection," objected Gerald. "I think it's highly unlikely that Sir Richard served twenty-five years in the King's Guards Regiment without upsetting quite a few powerful people himself. He might have created the passageway in case he needed to escape from his own enemies, not his wife's."

Brazelle wasn't so sure. "Perhaps, but that wouldn't explain why Sir Bernard retained that part of the basement of the old house when he had the Georgian mansion built more than a century later, and then created a second passageway connecting it to the new basement. On the other hand, if Lady Adeline really was the legitimate heir to the throne, then in turn that is what Sir Bernard would have become. And he might have thought it wise to maintain the escape route just in case he ever needed it himself. After him, as the family secret was passed down through the generations, it's likely that each subsequent heir would have seen it as sound policy to do the same. History shows that those who hold power can display extreme hostility towards any potential rival, especially those who have a much stronger claim to that power than they do. The Stuarts, the Hanoverians and the rest, all could have posed a threat if they ever became aware of the true ancestry of the Harfield family."

"Or perhaps maintaining the passageways simply became something of a family ritual," Gerald suggested. "Most families have their own quirky traditions. I know mine does. And how did the family manage to keep the secret to themselves for well over three hundred years? Although, from what you say, it doesn't appear that either Frances or Rose knows anything about it. And that also surprises me. Why didn't Sir Cornelius pass on the secret to Frances? As the eldest child she would be the next in line. And she was turned thirty by the time he died. I'm surprised he hadn't got round to passing on the family secrets by then. But all this is conjecture. To make the story even barely credible, you're going to need something tangible to back it up with."

"Just like you, I find it hard not to feel skeptical about it all," said Brazelle. "And even if the story isn't true it might still have been believed by the later Harfield generations. That could also explain why they might have continued to feel under threat and decided to maintain their escape route, all the way down to Sir Cornelius. On the other hand, if the story is true, there are quite a lot of other family mysteries that it explains."

Gerald was certainly right in one respect - it appeared that Sir Cornelius had not passed on the family secrets to either Rose or Frances. But Brazelle was growing increasingly convinced that he had passed them on to Gareth. But why did he do that? Brazelle could understand why Cornelius had not got round to telling Rose. After all, she was still only an infant at the time of his death. But why tell Gareth, a young boy, rather than his eldest daughter Frances, a mature woman? Cornelius was a highly intelligent man, a genius in fact, so surely he would have done nothing without reason. And if he'd confided in one person, was it possible he'd confided in anyone else? A close friend, maybe, someone he felt he could trust.

Brazelle took another swig of his whisky. "You told me a while back that your father and Sir Cornelius had been good friends for a very long time. I'm wondering how far back their friendship went and just how close they were."

Gerald smiled. "If you're asking that question for the reason I suspect that you might be, then I suggest you think again. Even if Cornelius did tell my father any of his family's secrets, which I very much doubt, he's never going to tell you about them. My father takes his promises of confidentiality extremely seriously. They first came across each other at a very early age, because they were both born and bred here in Prinsted. But Cornelius was more than ten years older than my father and their relationship didn't really start to develop until my father took over as the village doctor when his father retired."

Brazelle reacted with surprise. "I didn't know your family had provided the village doctors here in Prinsted for three generations."

"Oh, it's been a lot more than just three generations," said Gerald. "My family has supplied Prinsted with its medics since long before even the Harfields arrived. We go right back to the days when the treatment for just about any ailment was the skilful application of a leech, usually accompanied by some gibberish spoken in dog Latin, just to further impress and bewilder the patient. One of my father's abiding quips is that we Caulfields have been confounding, and bleeding dry, the good folk of Prinsted for centuries. According to family tradition, the first Caulfield medic arrived in Prinsted sometime in the early seventeenth century, but his surname wasn't Caulfield. He was a French Huguenot refugee called Alexander de Calvairac. It wasn't until the beginning of the nineteenth century that the family name was transformed into Caulfield. The change was prompted by the war with Napoleon, apparently. A lot of anti-French feeling developed around that time and presumably the family, who were well Anglicised by then, thought it might be prudent to remove any remaining vestiges of Frenchness. Probably not such a bad idea when you remember what happened to the monkey in Hartlepool.

Brazelle smiled. "So, would you describe the relationship that developed between Cornelius and your father as a close one?"

"Pretty much," said Caulfield. "But it wasn't one without its ups and downs. At some time in the distant past there was a bit of a falling out between the two of them. I have no idea what it was about, but it was serious enough to cause a rift that lasted a couple of years. Eventually, though, they seemed to patch things up and their relationship went back to what it had been before, more or less. If you want to know anymore you'd better ask my father yourself. Although I doubt he'll tell you very much. Would you like me to give him a call and say you'd like to meet him to ask for his advice? I won't tell him anymore, I'll leave that to you."

"Yes. I'd be grateful if you would do that," Brazelle replied. "Ask him how he's fixed about eleven o'clock tomorrow morning."

Day Eleven - Thursday

Gerald's father, Dr. James Caulfield, a widower in his late seventies, lives alone in a thatched stone cottage on the western edge of Prinsted village. The property has belonged to the Caulfield family since it was built in the early seventeenth century, although until Dr. Caulfield chose to spend a small fortune restoring it, before eventually moving to live there at the time of his retirement, it had been left in a semi-derelict condition for many years. At one time the sizeable plot on which the cottage stood had been completely surrounded by land belonging to the Harfield Estate. And it was identified as unique within the village, by being the only parcel of land that Sir Richard Harfield, the first Baronet, had never attempted to purchase. This feature of the property's history was fairly well known locally, although nobody was aware of an explanation for it.

Caulfield, a keen beekeeper, was in his garden tending to his hives when Brazelle arrived for their eleven o'clock meeting. Removing his apiarist's hat and gloves, he held out his hand to his visitor, before immediately launching into a lecture on the benefits of beekeeping. "It's a very rewarding activity, you know, Chris, and highly therapeutic. During my years as a GP I advised many of my patients to take it up for the good of their mental health. I even tried to persuade the Local Health Board to recommend to other General Practitioners that they might consider doing the same. I was convinced it would be far more effective than a lot of other, far more costly, therapies. They all thought I was mad of course, but then they were a bunch of ignorant and bigoted melissophobes. And honey has countless medicinal uses, you know. For a start, it's a highly efficacious antiseptic. My family has been involved in beekeeping and using honey to treat all manner of ailments for generations. Unfortunately, though, I haven't been able to convince Gerald to take an interest, so it looks like the centuries old Caulfield-apis mellifera relationship will come to an end with me."

Caulfield led the way into the lounge, which, as might be expected in a seventeenth-century stone cottage, was compact and snug with the fireplace its most prominent feature. A collection of family photographs was arranged along the deep mantelpiece and Brazelle's interest was taken by one in particular. It was a photograph of a couple on their wedding day. The bride was wearing a fairly traditional bridal gown and the groom was dressed in military uniform.

"Is that you?" asked Brazelle.

"Yes," Caulfield replied. "My late wife, Mary, and I got married just over forty years ago, when I was still in the Royal Army Medical Corps, hence the uniform. In fact that's how Mary and I met. She was a military nurse with the Queen Alexandra's. I joined up a couple of years after leaving medical school. Adventure. See the world. All that kind of stuff. I was in for eight years altogether and might have stayed in longer, but Mary was pregnant with Gerald and my father decided to retire. So I resigned my commission and took over from the old man back here in Prinsted. But you didn't come here to listen to my autobiography. Gerald said you wanted some advice from me. So, what is it, Chris? Is it medical advice you're after, or are you thinking of taking up beekeeping?"

"Neither. I've come about this." Brazelle handed Caulfield the letter he'd discovered hidden in Sir Cornelius' desk.

Caulfield studied it in silence for a few minutes, before walking over to the drinks cabinet, pouring himself a large whisky and offering one to his visitor.

"No thanks," said Brazelle. It's a bit early in the day for me."

"For me to," responded Caulfield, before taking a large swig and handing the letter back to Brazelle. "Where did you get this?"

"I found it in a hidden compartment in the desk in Sir Cornelius' studio," Brazelle replied. "I came across it by pure chance whilst looking for something else. Frances Marshall gave me permission to carry out the search, but she doesn't know I found the letter. Nobody does. I haven't mentioned it to anyone else, so you're the only person who knows I've got it. I'm hoping you can help me decide what I should do with it."

"You could burn it," said Caulfield, abruptly.

"Yes, I know," Brazelle responded. "And I did consider destroying it. But I didn't think it was my decision to make, at least not before getting some advice. And I thought you would be the best person to give that advice, seeing as how you were the person who wrote it."

Caulfield took a second swig of his whisky. "I'm sure it will be fairly obvious to you that it was written in reply to a letter that Cornelius sent to me. We hadn't had much contact over the previous couple of years, so getting a letter from him came as a bit of a surprise. Then reading what he'd written gave me an even bigger one. It was just a single question: 'Is it possible for a child who is Blood Group A, to be born to a mother who is Blood Group O, if the father is also Blood Group O'? It was an extremely odd question for Cornelius to have asked. For a start, although he wasn't a biologist, he would have had no difficulty quickly finding the answer for himself. He didn't need to ask me. In fact I'm sure he knew before he even sent his letter that the answer to his question was an emphatic, NO. It's a biological impossibility. The father would have to be Blood Group A or AB. Anyway, regardless of my certainty that he was already aware of all this, I decided to still send him a reply and answer his question. And that's the letter you've just found."

Brazelle had already concluded Caulfield's letter was written in reply to a question posed by Cornelius. And it was quite obvious from the nature of the reply what that question had been. But, why would Cornelius ask a question to which he already knew the answer? Especially asking it of a man from whom he appeared to have been somewhat estranged at the time? And what about Dr. Caulfield's role in this odd exercise? Why would he bother to send an answer when he was certain that Cornelius already knew what it was?

Brazelle never knew Cornelius when he was alive, but he was quite confident that he had got to know enough about him since becoming acquainted with the Harfield family, to very much doubt he would have done something without a reason. And he believed the same was true of Dr. James Caulfield. So, what was the reason for the exchange of letters? Brazelle guessed that Caulfield was unlikely to tell him, but he asked anyway.

"I can well understand your puzzlement, Chris," said Caulfield. "But I'm afraid you'll have to stay puzzled. So far I've only told you what you had probably already worked out from reading the letter you found. Anything else you get to know will not be from me. But let me add a word of caution, Chris. You're an intelligent chap and, Gerald tells me, also a very inquisitive one, someone who finds it difficult, impossible even, to leave a question unanswered. That can occasionally be a dangerous mix, when key bits of information are unavailable or sometimes even unknowable. In such circumstances when eager, or maybe even desperate, to come up with an answer it's not unusual to draw entirely the wrong conclusion. And trust me I know what I'm talking about. I was a good doctor and took my vocation very seriously, but not all my diagnoses turned out to be correct. And neither might yours be. So beware. I destroyed the letter that Cornelius sent me a long time ago. Until today I had assumed he'd done the same with my reply. Please trust me Chris when I say that nothing good will come from hanging on to that letter. I strongly suggest you burn it and then forget all about it. You came to ask for my advice and now you have it."

Brazelle only took fifty percent of Dr. Caulfield's advice. When he got home he destroyed the letter, but he would not be forgetting about it any time soon.

At exactly three o'clock in the afternoon, as punctual and bizarrely dressed as ever, Professor Simms arrived at Harfield House to return Adeline's portrait and deliver his expert verdict on the piece.

"Having completed the most detailed perlustration and carried out the most stringent analyses, I am of the very firm sentiment that the picture is, without the merest scintilla of incertitude, a genuine Kneller. Furthermore, its cornucopia of exclusive features, make it, in my humble opinion, the most wondrous of that species. And believe me, madam, I have seen them all."

Frances's face lit up, but before she had a chance to express her feeling of joy Professor Simms continued. "Regrettably, however, it is those same unique features that will prevent me from publicly endorsing the painting as genuine."

The expression on Frances's face changed dramatically. "Why ever not?" she exclaimed.

"For the simple reason, madam, that I cannot explain them," Simms replied. "Queen Henrietta Maria's wedding jewellery, the image of King Charles and the links to Catholicism. I am at a loss to explain the reason or justification for any of these inclusions. Even your assumed identity of the portrait's subject appears to be supported by only a very limited amount of circumstantial evidence. If I were to go public with my declaration of authenticity I would be immediately put under the most intense interrogation. My every pronouncement on the matter would be scrutinised to the nth degree by an army of self-opinionated art critics, not all of whom hold generous feelings towards me personally. Every aspect of the painting would be queried, not always in an open-minded way, and in many of those instances I foresee myself being unable to respond in my usual confident and informed manner. I fear I would be ripped to shreds in the bear-pit that poses as the fellowship of modern art criticism and my professional standing and career would be utterly destroyed."

Frances was understandably disappointed. At the same time she thought Professor Simms reaction was a little over-dramatic. "So, is that to be the end of the matter?" She asked.

"Not necessarily," Simms replied, offering a glimmer of hope. "If, at some time in the future, compelling evidence were to be found, explaining the inclusion of the unique features in the portrait to which I have alluded and, ideally, confirming the identity of its subject, then I would, of course, be willing to reconsider my decision."

Day Twelve - Friday

Brazelle rose early to spend a couple of hours on Rose's portrait and was making good progress when he received a phone-call from Frances. She started by reporting on Professor Simms' second visit and his refusal to publicly declare Adeline's portrait a genuine Kneller. She was somewhat puzzled when she sensed that Brazelle was perhaps not as disappointed at hearing the news as she herself was. But she made no comment on it. There were other more pressing matters she wanted to raise.

"I'm going to have to leave for the States later today," she said. "Damien's already on his way over there and he's asked me to put a few of his things together and follow him. There's a diplomatic crisis. I'm sure it'll all be over the news by lunchtime. Last night the British Ambassador in Washington shot himself. Lord knows why. It was only a few weeks ago we had dinner with him and his wife and he appeared in the best of spirits. Absolutely tragic."

"I'm truly sorry to hear that," said Brazelle. "It really is tragic when someone gets to the point where they end up committing suicide. Have you any idea how long you'll be gone for?"

"Not a clue," Frances replied. "But I'm sure it will be at least a month or two, whilst Damien holds things together over there. UK ambassador to the United States is one of the most important diplomatic jobs there is, so nobody's going to want to rush choosing the new appointee. In the meantime Damien will be under a lot of pressure, so I'll have to stay and support him. And I was so looking forward to Rose's return. I doubt we'll have a chance to meet up during the couple of days we'll overlap in the States, because we'll be in different cities and we'll both be so busy. And, of course, we'll have to put off your planned seminar on the contents of Sir Bernard's journals. I know you said they're not an easy read, but perhaps I could take them with me and have a go at reading through them myself. After a few days things should settle down a little, for me, that is, not for Damien, and then I could take a look at them."

Before going over to Harfield House to deliver the journals, Brazelle made another visit to the Harfield Estate Office. He found Lee Northcott in almost exactly the same position he was in the last time he'd called, his left leg still in plaster and up on the desk.

"I was passing and wondered if you had any more stuff that needed to be moved down to the strong-room," said Brazelle. "Or is there anything else I can help you with?"

"That's very kind of you Reverend. And as a matter of fact there are a couple of files that need to be stored away." Northcott pushed two folders across the desk and handed Brazelle the key to the strong-room.

Brazelle opened the door at the top of the basement staircase but didn't immediately go down. "Does everything in the strong-room belong to the Harfield family?" He asked.

"As far as I know," Northcott replied. "Why do you ask?"

Brazelle gave a shrug. "Just call it idle curiosity."

Down in the strong-room Brazelle placed the files he had just been given on top of those he'd deposited two days earlier. He then removed a package from inside his jacket and squeezed it into a small space he created behind a pile of some of the most ancient looking files, before covering it over with some other equally ancient looking bundles. It was all done in seconds.

Whenever Brazelle had spoken with Frances about Sir Bernard's journals he'd always referred to them in the plural, but never told her their exact number. It hadn't been a deliberate lack of precision, but it turned out to be a convenient one. When he arrived at Harfield House he handed Frances just two volumes. The last two.

Day Thirteen - Saturday

As anyone who has ever taken a professional risk knows, there is a thin line between initiative and insubordination. During Brazelle's years of military service it had been a line he had straddled on a number of occasions, but, for Chief Inspector Jenkins, it had recently been a new experience. Fortunately, thanks to the help he had received from Brazelle and Coyte-Sherman, when the dust settled, he found himself on the right side of it. No longer a fugitive, but now fully rehabilitated, with his professional status restored and his wounds pretty much healed up, he arrived at Holford dressed in his police uniform.

Although not the only reason for his visit, Jenkins was keen to express, face-to-face, his profound gratitude to Brazelle. "If it hadn't been for you and Daniel I don't know how things might have turned out. There was a good chance I could have ended up in jail, or, at the very least, been sacked for insubordination. As things now stand, though, I'm in line for a commendation and there's even the possibility of another quick promotion. I hope I get the chance to repay you and Daniel at some time in the future."

"It's a funny old world, isn't it," said Brazelle. "One minute they want to court-martial you and put you in chains. Then the wind changes and suddenly they want to give you a medal."

Jenkins gave a nod of agreement and moved to the second reason for his visit. "I've brought some news I thought you would want to hear. First off, there's some fresh info on the Triumvirate. Daniel got a call from his CIA contact early this morning to tell him all three members have now been located. But there isn't going to be any kind of trial."

"And why is that?" asked Brazelle.

"Because they're all dead," replied Jenkins. "They all killed themselves within twenty four hours of each other, before the FBI arrived to arrest them."

Brazelle was shocked. "What? All three of them?"

Jenkins gave a shrug. "That's how it appears. Daniel's CIA contact wouldn't give their names. He just said they were all male and politically well connected establishment figures. He reckons there'll be so much publicity given to their deaths, though, that we'll probably be able to work out who they are for ourselves. But their identities will never be publicly confirmed."

Brazelle's sense of shock shifted to cynical disbelief. "A bit too convenient, don't you think?"

"It did cross my mind," replied Jenkins, "And Daniel thinks the same. He reckons it's far more likely that once they were identified some black ops specialist was put on their case. Their deaths will certainly minimise the CIA's embarrassment."

"I think Danny's right," said Brazelle. "And it won't be just the CIA's embarrassment that'll be reduced. If I were a gambling man, I'd bet that a lot of other politically well connected establishment figures are giving a sigh of relief this morning. I reckon we're going to hear the phrase,

'I barely knew the guy', used quite a lot over the next few weeks."

"I'm sure you're right," Jenkins agreed. "And Daniel's CIA contact reckons that with the intelligence they're getting from Cotham and the others who have already been rounded up, it won't be long before all the remaining members are identified and the Triumvirate's organisation is completely destroyed."

Jenkins thought that Brazelle would also like to know that Julie's murder was now a closed case. "The senior investigating officer, the CPS and the coroner are all satisfied it was the ex-husband acting alone," he said. "Under normal circumstances he would have been one of the first people the investigating team would have wanted to interview, but circumstances were anything except normal of course. When my fingerprints were found at the murder scene and Leonardo identified me as the person who'd been trying to locate Julie just a few hours before she was killed, the investigating team saw it as pretty much an open and shut case. I was already a wanted man who was implicated in six other killings, so why not one more? It wasn't until after we'd caught Cotham and Grace McAllister they realised they'd been on a wild goose chase and started to rethink the whole case from the very beginning. Although you got to the ex-husband first they were actually only a few hours behind you. When did you realise it was him?"

"It was when I read some of the details reported in the newspapers," replied Brazelle. "I had a couple of advantages over the police investigating team, of course, which meant I could approach the case with an open mind from the very beginning. For a start, I knew that you were an innocent man. Secondly, you'd already passed on to me what Julie told you about herself. When I read the press reports, I thought it had all the hallmarks of an unpremeditated crime of passion, almost certainly carried out by a man. Women tend not to be stranglers. And the jealous ex-husband fitted the bill perfectly. I knew that the murderer in such cases, in a fit of remorse, very often kills himself soon afterwards, so I wasn't very surprised to find him dead when I paid him a visit. I used the local press to find out where he lived. They love a messy divorce and from what Julie told you it sounded like there'd been one. She told you she'd moved from Abingdon and gave an approximate date for her divorce, so I started with that. And by the way, you were right. It was a black Merc."

"I'm glad I managed to get that detail right," said Jenkins. "But there is one other detail that I can't explain. And neither can Daniel. Why were the mercenaries who attacked the safe-house kitted out with Met gear? Can you come up with a suggestion?"

"Not one that I have overwhelming confidence in," Brazelle replied. "But one thought has crossed my mind. Bringing armaments into the UK, particularly military grade weapons and ammunition, is extremely difficult, especially if you want to do it in a hurry. It's actually much easier to get your hands on hardware that's already here in the country. Provided you've got the money to pay for it, of course. One of the sources is the military. I know from my time in the army that every once in a while kit goes missing with some ending up on the criminal market. But you won't be reading about it in the papers. The military goes to great lengths to keep it hushed up. Another potential source is the police. As you well know, the Met in particular has an enormous stockpile of weaponry stored in various locations around the capital. I'd do a stock take if I were you."

Brazelle then changed the subject. "But on an entirely different matter - your offer to do me a favour - does it necessarily have to be something legal?"

Jenkins smiled. "I'd be prepared to go out on a limb and take a risk, like you did for me, if that's what you mean. But I'd prefer to stay out of jail. You sound like you might already have something in mind. Do you?"

Brazelle opened the door to the study. "Just give me a moment," he said. When he returned a few minutes later he handed Jenkins a sheet of paper. "You have access to personal information about individuals that I can't get hold of. Do you think you could get this for me?"

Jenkins read what was on the sheet before replying. "Probably, but I'll be sticking my neck out. It's the sort of personal information I'd normally need a good reason for accessing. What do you intend to do with it?"

"It's best I keep that to myself," Brazelle replied. "But rest assured I won't be using it for any kind of illegal purpose. And, if you don't mind, there is one other matter you might be able to help me with. You told me a while back that you have a first in law from a highly reputable university. How reputable?"

"Cambridge," Jenkins replied. "Is that reputable enough for you?"

Brazelle gave a shrug. "It'll do. I'm hoping you can help me out on a legal point. I want to know if a marriage is valid if one of the two parties involved is using an assumed name."

"It depends," Jenkins replied. "If it's with the intention of committing a crime, such as fraud, or if they had assumed someone else's identity, then the answer is no, it is definitely not valid. Otherwise it's probably okay. Legally you can call yourself anything you like, as long as you're not doing it with evil intent. Does that help?"

"Up to a point," Brazelle replied. "But I didn't know the law recognised the concept of evil."

"It doesn't. I was trying to put my answer into clergyman's language," said Jenkins. "Anyway, whose marriage have you got in mind?"

"It's the marriage between Justine and Sir Cornelius," replied Brazelle. "Do you think that marriage was legal?"

Jenkins was beginning to feel out of his depth. "That's a tricky one. I'll have an attempt at an answer, but I'm no expert, so it has to come with a disclaimer. Justine had assumed the identity of another person, albeit a dead one, and under normal circumstances that is very definitely illegal. Although it could be argued that she hadn't done it with the intention of committing a crime, it could equally well be argued that she'd done it in order to escape the legal consequences of crimes she'd already committed. On the other hand, she was also trying to remain hidden from some Italian gangsters. So it could be argued that she'd done it for reasons of self defence. It sounds like one of those cases that could end up in the Supreme Court. I think you'll need to consult a much higher legal authority than me. But why does it matter? Is someone showing an interest? If not, then I'd suggest letting sleeping dogs lie."

"I'm not aware that anyone other than me is showing an interest at the moment," said Brazelle. "But there's a chance that might change in the future. I'm thinking of the effect it would have on Rose if, at some time in the future, her parents' marriage was judged invalid. That would make her illegitimate in the eyes of the law. Wouldn't it?"

Jenkins gave a shrug. "Does that matter? She'd still be their daughter and surely that's the most important thing."

"Perhaps," said Brazelle.

Jenkins had one last task to complete before leaving. He went out into the yard and opened his car boot. This time, rather than a handcuffed prisoner, he removed a long thin package and handed it to Brazelle. "Daniel asked me to bring this along," he said. "It's a gift for Max from General Michaels." Brazelle guessed straight away what it might be.

"Just one last question before you go," said Brazelle. "Did Daniel's CIA contact say how and where the three members of the Triumvirate died?"

"Yes, he did. He said they all shot themselves," Jenkins replied, "two in New York and the other one in Washington."

Day Fourteen - Sunday

The last of the morning congregation had just left St Catharine's and Brazelle was about to return to Holford when an unexpected visitor arrived.

"I thought I might find you here," said Professor Davey. "I've just returned from France and felt sure you would welcome receiving an account of progress."

Davey, never a man for wasting time on small talk, got straight into his report. "The good news is that I have managed to locate the Bollezeele parish records for 1659, the year in question. They were stored in the archives of the Diocesan office in St Omer where they've been ever since March 1672. They were deposited there shortly after the death of Father Levesque who had been parish priest in Bollezeele for the previous thirty years. Even more good news is that Levesque appears to have been a model bureaucrat. I have no idea what his sermons were like, but I can confirm that his calligraphy and attention to detail in his record keeping were second to none."

"Something tells me there is a BUT coming," said Brazelle.

Davey put on a glum look. "You are very perceptive Mr. Brazelle. Unfortunately there is a BUT. And a fairly big one it is. The records are written in a collection of three volumes, with a page devoted to each of the three hundred and sixty months of Levesque's incumbency. And having myself inspected those volumes I can confirm that all but two of those pages are present."

"Let me guess," interrupted Brazelle. "The two that are missing are those for March and December of 1659."

Professor Davey nodded. "Sadly, yes."

"An odd coincidence, don't you think Professor?" said Brazelle. "The very two months that you went in search of. But how had they been removed? Did it look like they'd been roughly ripped out?"

Davey shook his head. "No, on the contrary, it appeared to me that they had been very carefully extracted. However, without giving the reasons for my interest, I raised the matter of the two missing pages with the archivist. She assured me there was no evidence to suggest that the volumes had been tampered with since they were first deposited in the archives. On the other hand, as far as I could ascertain, neither was there any evidence to prove that they had not been. Consequently, we are left with the conclusion that the missing pages could have been removed at almost any time since they were first written on."

Brazelle did not see the situation as hopeless. "The fact the pages were removed doesn't necessarily mean they were also destroyed. They may still exist. Although, having said that, I have no idea where to go looking for them next."

"And, regrettably, neither do I," said Davey. "It seems the matter is as much a mystery now as it was when you first brought it to my attention. One thing that has changed since that time, however, is the degree of plausibility I attach to the story. That, Mr. Brazelle, has risen enormously."

For the time being there was little either Davey or Brazelle could think of doing to make progress on the case, but they agreed to keep in touch and reconvene if something helpful cropped up.

Davey also agreed to keep the matter confidential. "I have no desire to risk starting a gold rush before I myself have first located the mother-load," he said.

Day Fifteen - Monday

Brazelle was working in his study when an email arrived from Jenkins providing the information he had asked for. After printing off a copy he went to pay Dr. James Caulfield a second visit and again found him in his garden tending to his beehives.

"I was wondering how long it would be before you returned," said Caulfield. "Gerald warned me that you find it almost impossible to let things go."

Brazelle's only response was to hand Caulfield the printed copy of Jenkins' email. The old man read it, before leading the way into his cottage, pouring himself a large whisky and offering one to Brazelle, which, on this occasion, he accepted.

"Whoever provided you with this information almost certainly breached official protocols and may have even committed a crime," said the old man. "But I won't waste my time asking where you got it, or who gave it to you. That would seem rather pointless. I'll just ask what you intend to do with it."

"Exactly what I did with your letter to Cornelius," Brazelle replied. "I shall destroy it."

"Then why on earth have you brought it here to show me?" asked Caulfield.

"Because it doesn't tell the whole story," Brazelle replied. "And I was hoping that you would fill in the gaps. I can well understand you thinking that none of this is any of my business, and in any other situation you would be right, but there are potential implications in this case that make it far more than just a private family matter. I believe that when Cornelius wrote you his letter, it wasn't to ask you a question, to which he already almost certainly knew the answer, but to send you a message. A message telling you that he had discovered he was not the biological father of one of his two daughters. I had already guessed that was probably the case, but this email, listing the blood group of everyone concerned, confirms it. And it also identifies the daughter."

Brazelle took a swig of his whisky before continuing. "But a very obvious question remains. Why did he send his message to you? Although you had been close friends in the past, at the time you received Cornelius' letter, you admitted yourself, you were estranged. And as the long standing Harfield family doctor with knowledge of the blood group of each of its members you would have already been aware of the biological impossibility of him having fathered one of his daughters. Cornelius knew all of this, so I can only think of one logical reason why he would have sent you that letter. And although this email doesn't prove I'm right, it certainly adds credibility to what I'm thinking."

Caulfield drained his glass and poured himself another large whisky before making a response. "Cornelius was a good man, possibly the best man I've ever known and certainly a much better man than me. Shortly after Brigitte, his first wife, died, whilst going through her things he discovered a letter. It was one she had written to me, but never actually sent. He confronted me with it and asked if it was true that I had had an affair with Brigitte during the early years of their marriage. To my eternal shame I lied. I denied that there had ever been anything between us. During her final few months Brigitte had been on extremely strong drugs and I suggested to him that they had been causing her to perhaps hallucinate and imagine things that had never happened. I could see he didn't believe me, but I stuck to my story. For some time afterwards I feared he would take the matter to the GMC and I might be struck off. Even though the relationship between me and Brigitte had lasted only a matter of days, she was my patient, and it would have been enough to have ended my medical career. In the event, Cornelius's only response was to end our friendship and cut me off socially. Our occasional evenings in Cromwell's Tavern where he would beat me at pool and his frequent invitations to dine at Harfield House came to an abrupt end. Then one day, out of the blue and totally unexpectedly, I received his letter. You're quite right, Chris, I already knew that I was Frances' biological father, but I had chosen to remain silent on the matter. To this day I try convincing myself that I did it for the good of all, but in truth I did it out of cowardice. My reply to Cornelius was the nearest I ever got to coming clean on the matter. For a few days after sending my reply I was worried about what might happen next, but then Cornelius turned up at my door one evening and asked if I wanted to go down to Cromwell's Tavern, have a few drinks and play a game of pool. And that was that. Nothing was ever mentioned about my affair with Brigitte, or the paternity of Frances and things quickly returned to the way they had been before. Something must have happened to lead Cornelius to forgive me, but to this day I have no idea what it was."

Brazelle thought he knew what it might have been. Cornelius had himself, in what he might have considered to be a moment of weakness, had the briefest of affairs with Megan Richards, his married housekeeper, resulting in the birth of Gareth. And, as far as Brazelle knew, he had chosen to remain silent on the matter. Neither, it seemed, had he ever been in a situation where he had had to decide whether or not to lie about it. Perhaps that whole experience had made Cornelius more understanding and forgiving of James Caulfield, his former friend. He may well have thought that to do otherwise would have been hypocrisy.

"So now you know the truth what do you intend to do with it?" asked Caulfield.

"Nothing," Brazelle replied. "I am quite sure that no good purpose would be served by me doing anything else. There is always the chance that the truth will come out by some other route, of course, but it won't be because of anything that I say or do."

Caulfield was left puzzled. "Then why did you go to all this trouble?"

"It's possible that one day Frances's paternity may be judged to be not just a private family matter, but a concern of legitimate public interest" Brazelle replied. "For that reason I wanted to get to the truth. I'm afraid I won't be able to tell you any more than that, at least not for the time being. And perhaps I never will."

It had been an extremely eventful couple of weeks. Gant was back in legal custody. And the criminal organisation to which he, Vincent Cotham and Grace McAllister had once belonged was now decapitated and in the process of being dismantled. Julie's murderer had been identified. And both Jenkins and Coyte-Sherman were now both able to return to their normal duties with the real prospect of preferment within their respective careers. Brazelle was back in possession of the Harfield Estate jeep and Max had had his beloved shotgun returned.

And several Harfield family mysteries had also been solved, although it had only come about through others, some even more extraordinary, being brought to light in the process. Frances' paternity, for example, was an issue of concern to Brazelle. The secret was safe with him, but what if someone else got to know the truth? And, of course, there was the most enduring Harfield family secret of them all. Brazelle failed to see a way forward to resolve that one, especially given the missing Bollezeele parish records, Professor Simms' refusal to publicly endorse Adeline's portrait and no sign of Queen Henrietta Maria's rubies, just the alleged revelation of Sir Richard's ninety-seven year old widow. What, if anything, should he tell the Harfield household of their connection to the Royal House of Stuart? And when, if ever, should he recover Sir Bernard's first journal from the strong-room of the Harfield Estate Office, so the Harfield family could read it for themselves? There was always a good reason to let some sleeping dogs lie, particularly if they resembled Cerberus, the many headed ferocious hound of Hades.

Despite such thoughts, however, Brazelle knew he could not let the matter just rest where it was. It was not in his nature to leave questions unanswered or mysteries unsolved. But it would have to rest for now. It was time to head off to Heathrow where Rose's plane would land in less than two hours.

"Your place or mine?" asked Rose, as they passed the 'Welcome to Prinsted' village sign.

"Yours," Brazelle replied. "There are a couple of things I want you to see."

On arrival at Harfield House, Brazelle took Rose straight to the library where there was a new painting hanging on either side of Justine's portrait. To the left was the portrait of Rose that Brazelle had only just completed and to the right was Kneller's portrait of Adeline.

"Wow!" exclaimed Rose, clearly impressed, before moving closer to get a better look at each of the two paintings in turn.

"Well, I recognise myself in the one on the left," she said. "But who's the broad with the bling?"

"A very good question," Brazelle replied. "Let me try to explain."

CENTRAL PARK, NEW YORK, 24 HOURS EARLIER

The Delacorte Musical Clock began to play its six o'clock theme, its last of the day. The sun was not far off setting as the last of the joggers, dog walkers and occasional Qigong exponents began to leave Central Park. Rose took a break from her own jogging and sat down alongside a white haired old lady on one of the benches. The pair acknowledged each other with an exchange of smiles.

"It's been another beautiful day," said the old lady.

"Yes, it certainly has been," Rose replied, before reaching over and touching the old lady gently on the arm to draw her attention to three rough looking men who were walking towards them. "And I hope nobody's going to try and ruin it," she added.

The old lady eyed the three men to make her own assessment. "Would you like me to deal with this, my dear, or shall I leave it to you?" she asked.

"You take care of it," Rose replied. "I've already had quite a bit of exercise today and still have to jog home."

The old lady unzipped the bag sitting on the bench beside her and placed her right hand inside.

The three men lined up a few feet in front of the two women. "Good evening, ladies," said the man standing in the middle. "If each of you would just hand over your purse, phone, watch, jewellery and any other valuables you have, then nobody will get hurt."

Rose looked the man square in the eye. "Are you three sure you know what you're getting yourselves into?"

The man pulled a switchblade knife from his pocket, pressed the button on the handle and a six inch blade appeared. "Shut up bitch. Just hand over your stuff."

Rose did not flinch but continued to stare at the man.

"Now, now, there's no need for language like that," said the old lady. "I have something in here that will take care of everything." She pulled her right hand out of her bag to reveal it was holding a semi-automatic pistol fitted with a silencer. She pointed it at the knifeman's stomach and the three men began to slowly back away, before eventually turning and running off.

"Which one had the knife and called you a bitch?" asked the old lady.

"The one in the red pants," Rose replied.

The old lady took aim and fired. The man wearing red pants dropped onto his knees, but eventually managed to pick himself up and, clutching his wounded backside, he hobbled off after his associates, leaving a bloody trail as he went.

"That's one lucky sonofabitch," said the old lady.

"Lucky!" exclaimed Rose. "You just shot the guy in the ass."

The old lady smiled. "I was aiming at his head! Don't you remember what Jerry and Perry taught you, Rose? If someone ever messes with you, make sure you send them on their way with a permanent reminder that it was definitely a bad idea. That experience might turn out to be very educational for all three of them."

"Like they've learned that next time they attempt to rob a couple of women in the park they should take a gun, not just a knife?" said Rose.

The old lady made no response, but simply cast Rose yet another smile. After removing the silencer from the revolver and putting both items back in her bag, she took out an envelope and handed it to Rose. "It's your usual fee, times three, of course. And the Director also asked me to give you his personal congratulations on another job well done. Well, three jobs actually, wasn't it?"

Rose refused to accept the envelope. "Tell the Director these three were on the house."

"As you wish, my dear," said the old lady, returning the envelope to her bag. "I must say, I was very surprised when the Director told me you'd decided to retire and that you'd only agreed to do these last three jobs because you had a personal interest. But then he told me you'd had a large inheritance confirmed and that you'd decided to settle in England, having fallen head over heels for some English priest, of all things. I have to say, I never saw that coming. When Jerry and Perry decided to retire and recommended you as their ideal replacement, not just to take over their martial arts school, but also their side job as well, to be honest, I did have my doubts. But they were so insistent that you were a natural. And as experience has clearly shown, they were absolutely right. I thought you'd keep going for at least as long as I have. Does your English priest know what you've been doing for the past few years?"

Rose shook her head. "No, I'm pretty sure he doesn't have a clue."

"Will you tell him?"

"I haven't made up my mind yet."

"If you do, won't he be inclined to take a dim view, especially being a priest?"

"He's not a typical priest," said Rose. "He has a very colourful past of his own. And as far as I'm aware he's told me everything about it. Perhaps I ought to do the same."

"So, that's the end of all this business for you then, my dear?" said the old lady.

"Not quite," Rose replied. "There's still just one loose end to be tied up. But that will have to wait until I get back to England. I'm heading off back there tomorrow."

The two women stood up and the old lady stretched out her arms to give Rose a hug. "Well, if it doesn't work out and you change your mind, or if you just miss us, you know where we are."

"Thanks, but I won't be back," said Rose, before turning and jogging away.

The white-haired old lady watched her go. "I'm not so sure," she whispered to herself.

Two weeks later, whilst on his way to court, Sir Ted Gant was assassinated by a sniper's bullet to the head. The identity of the killer was never determined.

Lightning Source UK Ltd.
Milton Keynes UK
UKHW012317060922
408453UK00003B/19